INTIMATE SECRETS

UNTOLD

A Saga of Hood Fetish

By Derrick and Latroya

Johnson

Printed in the United States of America

ISBN: 9781731540027

AUTHOR'S THOUGHTS

Change is something society speaks about but really don't understand. We say we want it, yet we condemn those that do it. I like to thank Allah for allowing me the opportunity, the wisdom, and the courage to fight against the odd, instead of accepting them. My wife, Latroya Peters Johnson and I attack this as a team, by taking the early street experiences and turning them into fictional tales, for many to enjoy. It's a blessing to be able to do something positive after so many years of negativity.

Learning who you are, what you want, and where you're going has a lot to do with becoming a man. To my wife, who has become the most important person in my life... We did it again and guess what we are going to keep doing it. I got me a down chick on my team, a Bonnie and Clyde thing. I shine, you shine, we shine, and it only gets better from here.

To all our supporters, thank you guys for challenging us because it makes us step up to the plate and eat!!!

May Allah Bless Us All/ As-SALAMU ALAYKUM

Peace and Blessings Be Upon You

Rosie Galvez was a beautiful woman, inside and out, but at this moment none of that could be seen. Her eyes were swollen and the dark blemishes around her sockets, made her face resemble a character from "The Walking Dead". She pressed against her cheekbone and bit into her lip to keep from screaming. Tears ran down her face from the pain. The bruises were showing no signs of healing and that amazed Rosie because this abuse happened days ago. Why she continued to endure punishment was beyond her wildest dreams. *Love can't make you this blind!* She told herself.

She desired better. She wanted better. She needed better. Rosie turned the faucet on and place her hands beneath the cold water. Splash after splash, she hated him more and more. Something had to be done, if she wanted to survive this relationship, alive. Rosie clicked the switch, turning the bathroom black. She opened the door and stepped in the hallway of their small house. Rosie paused and listened. His drunken nature to her. His thinking...his drinking...his abuse. She used her hands as guides as she traveled slowly down the hall.

This was her house, and all that she had, so every squeak and crack was known to her easily. The snores grew louder when she entered the room where her husband was sleeping. *Jualian Galvez!* Rosie studied him for a long period of time. How easy it would be to cut his throat. She wondered what it would feel like to press a knife deep in his chest, but she had to think about her only child. As good as it would feel, Rosie dismissed the thought and focused on the plan she'd formalized months ago. Inside the closet, she quickly grabbed the small amount of money and stuffed it in the bag full of clothes.

It was just enough for her and her son's trip. Rosie hurried because she couldn't stand another beating. What she packed would hold them until they reached America. She willed herself to move. Her flight was scheduled to leave in a few hours. There was no time to be afraid. She held her breath to calm her nerves. This was for her and her son. Rosie clenched her fist tight and push forward. This time she wouldn't turn back, like so many other times. Her life was derailed by what she considered love. No way would the same course be lived out by her son. His dreams were her dreams.

"Wake up mijo", Rosie whispered in his ear. She knew he was tired because all night they'd argued, while he watches

in terror. The cab was on its way. So, Rosie scooped him in her arms, and with her loose hand, she grabbed the bag and walked briskly to the front of the house... and outside. A knew beginning was waiting on them and it was her job to make sure they saw it.

CHAPTER ONE

MIKAL

Mikal Edwards, set behind his oversized production system, studying the three women. They stood in the sound booth like fresh polished china. Each person was different in their own way but equally precious. He shook his head because staring at them, for a long period of time, was an addiction within itself. Mikal slid one hand across his wavy hair cut. Today was a long day. His Oxford dress shirt was showing that. He bobbed his head casually to the beat. One of the singers seem more interested in him, then completing this song. Eye contact after eye contact told him this. Mikal smiled inwardly. It might make this a lot funnier! He winked at the lady, then adjusted his headphones so he could hear the music collaborate with the women voices.

Mikal was tired, and the artist were even more but the main-focus was finalizing this song. He wanted to show his appreciation to the label that signed him, Street Approved Records. This situation was similar too

DEF Jam acquiring Mr. Kanye West. The position carried a lot of weight and Mikal was a producer who wrote, sung, and created. Again, he listened. Before tapping a few buttons. Something was

wrong, and it was disturbing him. The track didn't sound right. It wasn't coexisting with the melody of the singers. Mikal made more highlights in the distance, steadied the drums and deepened the base. He wanted this funky as a Dr. Dre beat.

Suddenly the problem manifested. It wasn't him causing the problem but a few off notes. Now that had his undivided attention. Mikal killed the music. He was met with nervous stares. "Pamela, um, this ain't workin' ma. I need more passion, more attitude, more energy...and one of ya'll pushin' too hard." He shook his head. "Not gonna work. Relax and sing... now let's take it from the top. Try to sound as good as you look." Mikal winked a second time. Pamela was the lead singer. Her voice was strong and the body that came with it was breathtaking. People saw her as the next Mariah Carey, but her work ethics was stopping her from making it to the top. He'd found her and the other women during a talent search. With them willing to work together, Secret Confessions was formed. No doubt, there was many secrets to be revealed.

Pamela, Moni, and Rachael! All different shades of colors. Seeing them was hypnotic and either one you choose was a good choice. Pamela, now, had his attention. She possessed a lot of spunk. That was something he liked.

Wrinkles formed in her forehead, as she stared through the soundproof glass, at him, Mikal pressed the intercom. "Pam is somethin' wrong?"

Her sexy pout covered her face. He could tell she was used to having her way. Pam toyed with her hair, before speaking. "I'm tired...this is our eighth session and you keep finding something to complain about. Why can't we finish tomorrow and maybe you'll hear it clearer". She replaced her words with a smile. Mikal looked at her long and hard. He wanted his statement to be gentle but firm. It was something about brats that he hated. They thought life was peaches and cream. He ponders over his thoughts awhile longer. This had to be played correctly. "Pamela, in order, to become Beyoncé, you must work like Beyoncé. No one said this would be easy. Now... if this ain't what you want, step aside and allow Moni to take your spot. Your free to leave." No one moved. "Well, in that case, one more time. Act like this is what you want, please."

The brief motivation speech served its purpose. Every missed tone came alive, Mikal smirked. "That's what the fuck I'm talkin' about!" he yelled in excitement and blew a kiss toward the women, to show his approval.

They stood in the lobby, waiting on their limo to arrive. The ladies wore full length chinchilla coats. They were the next to come. Moni was slender with a nice figure. It showed she stayed in the gym. Japanese and black was her nationality, with olive eyes filled of mischievous secrets. She watches but said little. Rachael, on the other hand, was the finest of the three. She was an amplified version of Johnny Blaze. On her, there was more ass and breast than a man knew what to do with. That wasn't the only attraction. She was gorgeous and gave no hint of it. Alicia keys reincarnated. Something every man wanted.

Pamela was like so many of the women he'd met before. Hot and not afraid of using it. She stood close to him, as they waited. Mikal whispered in her ear and received a giggle in return. Tonight, he planned on seeing how big of a freak she was. Thinking about it made his penis hard. That was his biggest problem. He loves having sex. They stepped into chilly December night and entered the vehicle. "Larry, take them to their suite downtown. These ladies are exhausted. Then I'm heading home." The driver nodded and drove toward the freeway.

Several times he'd thought about dealing with Pam but that always got him in trouble. Women didn't know how to accept good sex and move on. Still he went against his

words. Secret Confessions was his goldmine, but good pussy was his weakness. "Um, Mikal... I'm not going there tonight." Moni said. Surprised filled with his face. "Then where would you like to go?"

"Home with you." She replied.

Mikal laughed. Any other time, he would've jumped at the opportunity but his urge to sex Pamela was taking over. "That sounds good but- "

"Pam can come too." Moni glanced towards the other chick. "That's if she doesn't mind?"

Now this should be interesting! Mikal thought while he waited on her answer. His grin was taking over his whole face. *Life can't be this good!*

Pam chuckled. "Secret Confessions, I guess all of those will come out tonight." The ladies stared at each other.

"No need to be a party pooper. I've always wanted to sleep in a famous man's house." Rachael smiled, showing perfect teeth. Everyone laughed. Mikal opened the console and retrieved a bottle of Ace of Spade. "No need to wait. Let's get the party started now because from the looks of it, there want be much sleep tonight." More laughs. This was the life he wanted. A world with limited worries and lots of enjoyments. How could a man fuss? "Larry take us straight to my place."

The rays of dawn emphasized the muscles in Mikal's back, as he sat at the marble bench, of his piano. He Hummed a few notes, while tapping keys to match his rhythm. His voice was beautiful, but Mikal had no passion for singing. Why, he couldn't understand. The real love laid in the creative aspect of music. Seeing his vision come alive, was the satisfaction, he craved. The search for people to fit his sight, excited him. Mikal was 230 pounds and stood at 6'5, mixed with an ebony skin tone, tilted the game towards him. It gave a new meaning to tall, dark, and handsome. Doors open for Mikal because of his appearance but it always impressed people that he spoke three different languages: French, English, and Spanish. When he talked, people listened. More so, the sight of emerald green eyes, connected to a man with his hue, puzzled both sexes. That creole bloodline, thanks to his parents.

The thought of them brought about frustration. Their relationship was destroyed because of a heated argument pertaining to his sister. He blamed them for her death. Mikal closed his eyes and started humming again. *Hidden Love!* The name was painting a picture across his soul. No matter the number of women that accompanied his bed, what he longed for, never came. A soft hand rubbed his shoulder, causing him to glance backwards. *Moni!* She caressed his neck and then down the center of his back. She was amazing. Her body was covered only in lace panties, leaving her breast exposed. *Damn!* Mikal thought. Moni was the envisioned. Mikal began playing. "What are you doing?" she asked. "Working on a song."

Moni leaned closer and curled her arms around him gently. The smell of her Chanel perfume consumed him. "What's the name?" Moni asked, pressing her body closer.

Mikal took a deep breath. *If only you knew!* Hidden Love...here. He handed her the words on a piece of paper. "I'll take the first bars and you take the next ones. I just wanna see what we create." Then, he begins to sing. The search for love/ has always made me happy/ cause, I don't wanna be alone, no more." Moni's voice grabbed the air effortless. "And love will always be my desire/ until I bring you home to me, enjoying love is our destiny."

Mikal smiled, Silently, he prayed that neither one of the other ladies would be awake. Moni was single handed adding emotion to this song. That's what it needed. "So, let me love you tonight/ this is only the beginning of our life. Chorus Moni." He instructed.

"Single, kisses belong to you/ with a single life of truth/ but we'll never know/ 'till we open up the door...to this Hidden Love." Moni's, alto sound, made him stare longer then he intended. She had to sing this song. It was made for her. Mikal listened as she repeated the chorus. Gosh she's good! This was nothing like the woman in bed last night. There she was wild, crazy and dominate. Here, Moni was passionate, loving and caring. Mikal continued to listen until he could take it no longer. Slowly, he pulled her into his arms, allowing his large frame to engulf her. "I need you baby."

"Me too." Moni replied as her body was lowered on top of the cool piano.

Section after section his tongue traveled down her chest, until it touched the fabric of her panties. There he placed his face in the warmth of her vagina. He moved them aside and begin tongue teasing her. The arch in her back told him he was doing the right thing. A small scream escaped her mouth when he parted her pussy lips. "Take me pleaseeeee." Moisture was in Moni's eyes. She was at the point of no return. Mikal followed instructions. At this moment, she was the only woman he wanted. She was his Hidden love.

Mikal closed his eyes, as her golden legs twisted around him. They both was in search of the love they'd never experienced. Together, this morning, they'd found it but only for a short time. He made love to Moni like there was no other.

CHAPTER TWO

CANDICE

"That's it! Now turn left. Right there, right there! Give me a pout? Yes, yes beautiful baby beautiful! If you could only see you through my eyes, then you'd understand how marvelous you look." Candice held her breast in both hands, allowing the straps to her Simi swimwear bikini suit, to hang loose. She glanced over her shoulder, as flash from the cameras, brightened the room like stars in the night. Her focus was on the instructions given to her. The room was filled to its capacity, but no one was present in her mind. Nevertheless, they came to see Candi.

Candice Galvez was a 29 yrs. old Puerto Rican model raised in Brooklyn, NY. She was also a backup dancer, who'd performed with many of the elite. Her well portioned body was stacked. Candice stood 5'8 145 with 38-24-39 measurements. Her hair was pulled to the top and hung loosely over her face. This gave off the sex appeal men liked. Every selection of makeup sat flawlessly, [on her skin.] The red Christian Dior Ultra gloss was penciled in with perfection, giving her smile a touch of elegance. Candi turned, then paused. The see through, fabric of her bikini, brought extra attention to the rose vines entwined around her thighs. Red peddles, rest softly on the small of her back and along her 4" waistline. "Candi bite your nail devilishly. Drop the top! I want it to look like your guarding yourself from Satan himself. Yes, wonderful! Expose just enough...Yes! These people are witnessing history, in the making." The photographer yelled. Her features were enhanced with every snap of the cameras.

She was a born natural. To see her move was a blessing concealed. Her long legs strolled gracefully across the stage. Step by step she became more priceless. There wasn't many who possessed the same gift. "Turn baby...Now look off in the distance. Beautiful!" This was her reality. A dream she'd worked hard to achieve.

HOURS LATER...

Candace stepped out the shower and posted in front of the mirror. She examined her body. Beau ideal stared back at her, but it came at a cost. Water dripped down the center of her chest, over her naval and towards her light brown pubic hairs. Candice was impressed by the way things turned out. She dried slowly and covered herself with a thick cotton robe. A petite man studied her when she entered the room. "So, what do you think Melvin?" Her condo was uniquely furnished. Classic couches surrounded with mahogany wood tables showed she was dealing individuals that had money.

Melvin crossed, then re-crossed his leg. At 5'4, the act seemed humorous, but he did it effortlessly. Candice was his client and longtime friend. Their relationship consisted of back and forth agony, but she loved him to death. "Well." Melvin began. "There's talk about how awesome you were and that's something I agree with. You were soooo stunning...like wow."

That made Candace laugh. "That's a compliment, coming from someone who likes men." "The more the merrier." Melvin winked. She shook her head. Sometimes he could be extremely gay, and at times like that, Candice left him alone. He grabbed his half-filled glass of vodka and twirled the ice before taking a swallow.

There was something he wanted to say, and Candice could detect it. "Talk to me Melly!" She ordered. He smiled. "Am I that obvious?" Candice grinned. They were broken pieces of the same puzzle. Melvin said. "Candi you can dance and your beautiful but there's a lot people in Hollywood that have the same gift. We have to figure out how to separate you from the rest."

Candace frowned. Melvin stayed silent, to allow her time to release the frustration. "What I mean is, don't leave any stones unturnt. The gifts you have can only take you so far...And from what I seen, straight to a rich man's bed." "Fuck you Melvin!" Candice said. She got up and walked toward the window. His words hurt because they carried truth with them.

All the hard work wasn't getting her anywhere. Every road she traveled only ended with construction signs. Something always had to be fixed. "So, mister smart ass, what's the plan?" Melvin sat his glass down and stared into her eyes. *Hell, of a woman!* "This is strange. No fussing, no silly demands, no nothing." He rolled his eyes toward the ceiling. "This isn't the sweet Candi I know is something wrong darling?" A look of discuss rested on her face. "Speak Melvin...No time for games...Any of that childish shit."

Melvin nodded. The look she carried told him to walk light on the teasing. He rubbed his chin. *This just might work!* "Well, you need to add something else to that beauty. Something like singing, acting...

Something more."

"Adding something, will it work?" Candice asked. Melvin shrugged his shoulders. "Looks are everything in Hollywood but the accessories are what make you look worth it. You have too, take them by storm. J-Lo couldn't sing very good but look what she did. It's worth a shot, darling."

"What do you know?" Candice narrowed her eyes.

Again, Melvin giggled. They had so many secrets. All came in the last ten years. At 19 yrs. old they became inseparable. That was the year her mother died from cancer. "There's a talent search in Dallas, Tx on December 28th and Street Approved Records is heading it. So many artists will be there... but the owner is strict. Kimberly is her name and she's not accepting any free lancers. No invitations, no entrance. First thing in the morning, I'll see what I can do. Meantime you need to figure out what you're going to do because there's going to be a lot of bitches like you there." Melvin looked at her. "It shouldn't be hard. Your voice is like T-Boz of TLC. With a little work, this could be your chance." Candice smiled, giving her beauty mark on the side of her lip, the glow of the sun. Years of work could finally pay off. Candace thought. "Melvin make it happen and I won't disappoint." Her soft enhance lips, pecked him on the forehead. "I'm going to sleep...don't be up to late."

Candice stepped out of the snow and into the hotel lobby of the Shelton Inn. Her slim frame was covered with a dark romance Marc Jacobs coat that wore hand print taboo painting. She stood still for a second until her body adjusted to the heat surrounding her. The short venture, in the early winter weather, was torture on her bones. Candace removed her sunglasses and walked to the receptionist desk. "I'm here to meet Dr. Kofi Siriboe. Can you notify him I'm here please?" One call and she was entering the dimly lit room where the man she despised was at. She removed her coat to expose a sexy Hollister top, style Mafia pants, Steve Madden pumps and a Fauria hand bag.

"Candi it's always a pleasure to see you. I brought Ms. Johnson along being how you two get along so well." Mr. Siriboe joked. He understood their exchange between each other. The woman was completely flawless. Her vanilla skin tone resembles Halle Berry. The only difference, she was taller. Ebonie was 5'9 and 6'0 with heels. Every surgical repair a person could have was done on her. Exactly the reason Candice was here. Dr. Siriboe preferred to do private checkups on "special" patients. Today, he was examining her breast. Even though she disliked the woman, Candice put up no resistance. "No, Marlon, Ebonie's fine...a blessing in the making." They both knew it was a lie.

Ebonie Johnson was Dr. Siriboe's secretary and knew more about her business then Candice deemed respectable. With that, she crossed her fingers and moved forward. Kofi was a pervert and Candice hated being around him, but he was the best in the business, so those feelings had to subside. "Remove your shirt." Kofi squeezed lubricate in the palm of his hand and rubbed them together. Once her breast was visual, he cuffed them and massaged them for a long period of time. To long for any doctor to be examining for defaults. His not so handsome German features sent chills through her body. The money he made kept him in the class of presentable. Candice looked away to hide her disgust. Ebonie smiled just to add to her discomfort. Those was the games she played.

Dr. Siriboe removed his hands and smiled at Candice. "No lumps...and they feel great. This may be the best job I've done. How did they look Ebonie?"

"Your work always comes out good but thinking about what you started with... this maybe the best." Ebonie gave an approving smile. "It doesn't get any better." Candice rearranged her top before speaking. "Thank you." She glanced quickly away. "That was your last operation. It was a pleasure. Believe me, every time I see you grace the magazine cover, I smile because I know I was a part of that." Kofi stopped talking and studied Candice. "Is there something wrong?"

"No, no not at all, I'm thinking. Don't mind me. Can you order room service...? I haven't had breakfast this morning." Candice thoughts drifted again. *How can it be done!*

She prayed this was their last meeting. The man was a borderline sicko. Every time they met, he wanted to examine a different part of her body. That was his way of getting a cheap thrill, but that had to stop now. His fetish was becoming unbearable. "Is there ever a

time I can see you alone? In an environment like this."
Candice looked around the expensive suite. "As a matter
of fact, it is... maybe test those goods." Kofi laughed at
his own joke. Candice sat next to him and whispered in
his ear. "Make it happen and that may be the case. I
have special plans, but you know." She gave a shrug. Kofi
clamped his fingers together. "Will do."

CHAPTER THREE

MIKAL

If you hear a voice within you that says you cannot paint, then by all mean's paint and that voice will be silenced! Mikal's father's words repeated themselves in his head, as he walked. He painted when no one else liked his visions. Years later, the colorful picture came to life, like the priceless Mona Lisa. Sometimes getting away enables you to collect your thoughts and focus on the distractions around you. There is always warning before destruction; the roads become bumpy, branches fall, caution signs are avoided, but how do you overcome it?

No one wants to fail so what tactics do you take to accomplish more from life? "Redefine yourself." Mikal answered out loud.

Looking at the question with face value, could only determine what your life was really, worth. Mikal inhaled deeply, then tucked his hands inside his tailormade Burberry coat. The air was cool outside; almost relaxing to the point, of allowing his mind to drift in and out of his present reality. Christmas was coming, and Mikal still was unsure if he would visit his parents, this year. The house he had bought them was the place of gathering. *We can easily forgive a child that is, scared of the dark, but the real problem is when men are afraid of the light!*

Now, those statements gave him security, where he lacked. Their true meaning only registers once you have lived.

Birds chirped overhead, singing joyous songs of happiness. Mikal stood and listened to their sound. No stress, no worries, no problems. Even with all the success, his heart held emptiness. A king is only half a

King, when there's no queen to share his throne. Ashley was the only queen he knew. He'd promised to protect her but failed. Knowing that, failure was erased from his vocabulary. Mikal gritted his teeth and continued his walk along the rocky pavement. He stared in the distance; where snow rested on the mountain peaks. Seeing it made him smile. Yellowstone National Park was a place his family visited, often, when he was younger. Those were the peaceful times.

The business trip he'd set out for had become, an escape. Mikal looked over the large trees, hoping nothing was camouflaged between their leaves. Once he was assured, Mikal sat down on a medium size boulder, and begin meditating. His clothes looked out of place; Black on black, Louis Vuitton everything. Turtleneck, flat-front pants, and street boots. The only thing at this moment he appreciated was the boots. Dealing with his spontaneous personality, Mikal was glad he'd chosen them. Here he was in an absurd place, when this was a talent search trip. *Business first!* He told himself. Now he had to reschedule his flight, out of Wyoming, for the morning, because of a walk in the park. The strangest part about it was he felt at peace and that's what life was all about.

He rubbed his clean shaved face and focused on the rusty colored trees. He could tell they were beginning to die. The pine attached to the loose branches clung a hold to the needles embedded in its bark. Disaster was threatening to destroy their home. Mikal closed his eyes and thought back five years ago, when he was twenty-five, a time he would never forget...

"Dad where are we going?' Ashley asked impatiently. She was eighteen years old and excited to be out of high school. As gifted as she was, her looks often time's overpowered how smart she was. She resembled her mother so much; they could pass for sisters. At 5'2, the only thing that separated them was her complexion. Ashley had her father's light skin. Mikal took after Sabrina with a midnight hue. "It's a surprise. Go wait in the car, please." Carl Edwards wined.

Sabrina giggled. She was still as beautiful as her late graduation pictures. At that time, people compared her to the likes of Rutina Wesley. "Now you know that ain't going to happen."

With that statement, she turned her attention towards her son. "Mikal are you sure you don't want to go with us?" Sabrina rolled her eyes in the directions of them. "Those two are going to drive me crazy. You're my comfort." She grabbed a light jacket and tossed it across her wrist. His parents had a twenty-year marriage, and both continued to look at one another like the first day they'd laid eyes on each other. That told, all that needing to be said, especially with them being in their fifties. "No thanks ma. I must get this demo together and shoot this contract back before time run out. These people mean business. You can bring me back somethin' though... if that ain't a problem?" Mikal smiled.

Sabrina smiled back. He was her heart. Lightly, she placed a hand on his cheek. "It's not. Keep working son. Things will get better... what's the name of that label again?"

"Street Approved Records, they're the hottest thing jumpin' in Dallas right now. This may be the chance of a life time. I just have to show them what I can do."

His mother nodded. Then a horn blew in the distance. "Let me go before your father run my blood pressure up?" The horn sounded a second time. "Alright, alright already... keep working baby." She opened the door to a loud popping noise and moments later another. Sabrina stood frozen, screaming, with her hands pressed against her chest. Mikal was no dummy. He jumped to his feet and rushed passed her, into their driveway. On the ground, in a pool of blood, was his sister. He could see two men vanishing in the night. Mikal looked at his father with a questioning stare. He looked at Ashley and knew she was dead, but that would be hard to explain to his mother, who was kneeling next to her, holding her head in a death grip.

Mikal watched his mother cry. "The police are coming and..." Carl's sentence was shortened by Mikal's voice. "WHAT HAPPIN TO ASHLEY!" Anger, frustration, and sadness overwhelmed him. He wanted to act out violently, but this was his father.

"They were; they were here..." his words faded off.

Between shallow sobs, Sabrina spoke. "Carl, I told you not to get involved with them. It'll only bring trouble ...now look." She lifted her head up. "You should've just paid them."

"Paid who! Involved with who!" Mikal stood up. His 6'5 frame engulfing his father's smaller body, as his father begins to cry. "She jumped in front of me... they were after... I'm sorry." He dropped to his knees next to his wife. Mikal had no sympathy. Ashley was still dead.

That was the last time he had contact with his parents. It was hard to forgive them for his sister murder. They were both school teachers, that had enough sense to know, not to get involved with illegal activities. No matter how much debts they had. Not having patience to overcome their situation prove to be fatal and a stoppage for bridging their broken relationship. Mikal loved them never the less and to show that, he bought them a house and added six figures to their bank account. No thank you, no calls, no nothing in return. Even though the hurt was buried between his chest, Mikal loved his parents. He started back downhill. Avoiding the forest ranger's advice would only bring unwanted problems. He removed his phone and dialed. Tonight, he would stay in a hotel, but he would not stay there alone. Hello Mykitha. I've decided to wait till the mornin'." Mikal laughed. "Is that so. I'm at the Hilton, on the tenth floor."

Mikal entered the building, of his label and hustled towards his office. There was a lot of music to be produced. Secret Confessions was scheduled to be in the studio late this week and a new rapper name DamnFool, which was a head act for the Triple D. "Excuse me Mr. Edwards." A male secretary called out. Mikal stopped and turned to face the man. "Kim asked to see you as soon as you arrived. She's waitin' in her office at this moment." Mikal nodded and started walking down the long hallway. *What could this be about!* Mikal asked himself. Solo conferences were not her thing, so something important had to be on deck. He could think of only three time's that he was secluded with Kimberly and that was in the last five years. Her past was known to everyone that worked for the label, but no one dared speak of it. She was a big woman; even with her petite size.

The woman had a mean side to her and she could end your career before it started. From afar, Mikal admired her. Kim was one powerful person. She did not let her looks get in the way of business. Knock! Knock! Knock!

"Come in Mikal." Kimberly said. He walked in and looked around. It was hard to believe this office was designed the same way, the former owner Viper, had modeled it. The mans influenced ways, still was strong. "Have a seat please. I need to discuss my future plan's, with you." Kimberly winked, as she let down her hair. Mikal smiled. This was new! She recommended. "I've sent invitations out for people to attend our, Street Approved Records party." Kim made air quotations with her fingers. "I want you to find me a woman that can go in straight competition with Rihanna."

Laughter erupted from his mouth. Mikal continued until he noticed she was not joining in. "So how do you want me to do that?"

"I'm glad you find this funny." Kim said. "Your very handsome and you tend to catch some of the most exotic women I've seen. Hell, with those eyes, I can't say I blame them at all."

Mikal stared back. There were smoke signals in the air, but a scary line that was drawn; employee and boss. Kimberly cleared her throat; while busying herself with the papers in front of her, on the desk. "There's a big bonus, if you can pull this off. With your skills, you can make anyone a star. Another thing, Tracy wants to meet you. I've told him a lot about you and how you've helped keep this ship sailin'. He should be free Christmas. The Miami Heat don't play that day."

Mikal shook his head. "Is there a problem?" Kimberly asked.

"Just like that I'm on the spot, huh? Tracy comin' too?" He replied. "Just like that. This is how the big league go. You make moves and make money." She winked at him again. Mikal stood up and adjusted his coat. It was starting to get hot. 'I'll do my best. The way your actin',

I'd think I was some type of sex symbol." A soft chuckle followed the statement. Kimberly raised up, exposing her sexy body, for the first time that day. Chanel fitted jeans, stuffed inside white Chanel boots, was the only thing he could see. The loose blouse, connected with gold chains, never made it to his eyes. That alone had Mikal in awe. Kimberly examined him openly; she stepped closer and took in his smell. "Dior, one of my favorites." She brushed the imaginary lent off his chest. "You are... in more ways than you understand." Mikal moved the loose hair from around her ear and leaned in for a kiss. Kimberly smiled but placed a finger between them, on his lips. "Maybe one day but not now. I'm still working. I can't have you causing distractions. Business always first."

She traced her finger around his lips and down his jaw lining; then stepped away. They stared at each other for a while. "I'll see what I can do." Mikal turned and left her office.

CHAPTER FOUR

CANDICE

Early December cold fronts was controlling all activities through the state of New York. Candice pulled her thick trench coat close as she stumped quickly across Stone Street. This was a popular eating section during the year but now sat empty. She stopped and surveyed the scene, noticing nobody occupied any of the tables. Dark windows reflected images of metal staircases, light poles and scattered people, that was taking a heavy beating from the wind pounding against them. Candice crammed her neck tighter in her coat and hurried towards the entrance of THE DUBLINER. Mother Nature was handling everything on the outside of these walls.

She entered the dimly lit lounge and search over its comfortable setting. Staggered couples conversed in different sections. No one noticed her, even when she removed her coat and allowed the temperature to adjust with her body. She held her ground exposing a well-kept frame. More of her legs showed then most people in this type of weather. The romantic blouse was see through, and a glimpse of her bra could be seen. Her blouse hung loosely over the high cut leather Scuba skirt. Vanessa suede pumps enclosed her feet, giving her five eight-inch height an edge of six even. She was oblivious to the glances shot her way because they happened all the time.

A hand flash drew her attention toward the back table, where the individual, she was there to meet sat. She slowly sashayed in that direction. Importance could be seen with every step taken. Candice stopped and raked her fingers through the long locks in her head. "Kofi what a pleasure to see you again. Alone I should say. Unfortunately, the weather is horrible for anything else." Her Puerto Rican accent filled the air. "We are here to talk, right?" Candice set next to the doctor, not allowing him the opportunity to get her chair.

Dr. Kofi Siriboe nodded his understanding. "Don't be so prideful. At least accept a drink to warm your bones." Candace batted her eyes sarcastically but agreed. Kofi recommended. "A hot cocoa with whip cream should do the trick and it's easy on the body when winding down. Plus, I have more information while we wait on our orders." He waved his hand for service. Once done, Kofi studied her over the top of his glasses.

For the past year Dr. Kofi Siriboe had become more and more intrigued by this woman. There was so much a man would stand to gain from having a woman of her caliber. A simple smile crested his lips. When their orders arrived, he spoke. "After all the surgeries, you do understand that there is no chance of you becoming pregnant?" Kofi looked away frim her piercing stare. It felt like it was stabbing through his soul. "Thought I should bring it up."

Disgust was painted all over Candice's face. She knew the cost of her decision but to hear it openly made the pain cut deeper. "It's a price I'm willing to pay. Thank you for the reminder." They held eye contact longer than necessary. She watched the hidden lust sitting behind his eyes and that made her hate stronger.

Candice smiled with ease. This was part of her generic makeup. She was a part time actor and fulltime movie star, so it was a must she stayed on stage. Everything would end tonight. This was the reason for the visit. "How would you feel about spending the night with me?" Before Kofi could answer, Candice knew his response. Dark eyes, semi-bald head and homely face shined like he was being elected for president. Seeing that, assured her that the next move arises. The man knew too much. He could ruin everything with one press conference. Kofi's eye brows perked up with the thought of him laying between her sexy legs. Those dark eyes quickly did an in-take of the 34DD breast in front of him. *Such a man!* Candice told herself.

Instead of answering, Kofi leaned back in his chair and chuckled lightly. He held his cup with both hands. "Why the sudden change of heart?" His lust was still visual.

Candice pressed her lips together to smooth out her lipstick. Then she flicked her tongue across them for moisture. She watches him carefully. At that moment, Kofi's hand laid in his lap squeezing the bulge inside his pants. Candice watched candidly but said nothing. She wanted him to feel comfortable. "Does it matter? I'm focused on what we can accomplish." No emotions showed. "Now you can refuse but I promise I'll find another toy soldier." Her stunning smile enhanced the beautiful set of teeth she displayed.

Nothing was said between them. Both chose to enjoy their hot liquid in silence. She had no doubt in her mind that he would agree. Candice opened her legs wide enough for him to get a brief look at the white thong, before crossing them again. Her moves were calculated step by step. "You know you want it!" Candice repeated to herself. Kofi grabbed his key ring from the middle of the table and then swallowed the last of his drink, before standing. "I've always wanted a beautiful vixen next to me. Something foreign always seems fun." Kofi looked at her in a propitious way. "Terrace Garden isn't far from here. I think we'll be out the weather for the night." Candice laughed at his try for humor. She stood, slid on her coat and hooked an arm around his. "Hopefully this is what you've dreamed of."

He kissed along her breast, using his hands to massage her nipples. Candice arched her back to allow his tongue more skin to explore. Short gasps of pleasure escaped her lips while she rubbed against his body. One finger rested in her mouth, as the other caressed the lower end of his back. Kofi's head moved along her body and found every sensitive spot. He bit softly on her hip causing her to open those sexy legs wider. She wanted him to pound her body to make her remember this moment of humiliation. Kofi gentle lips sucked hard against her vagina. She pushed her body into him as he continued to tongue her insides. It was surprising how her body was responding.

The clicks of Candice's pumps were the only thing that could be heard in the night. She ran as fast as her feet would carry her. Every corner she turned, there was the same thought. Candice tried to get as far as away from the area as possible. Her nerves were shocked. She called several times to reach Melvin but was unsuccessful. Candice slipped inside a breezeway and dialed again.

Candice chest pressed against the bed while her face looked back. She felt his penis moving fast inside her. His hands cuffed her buttocks firmly, pushing them forward for a deeper thrust. All of him she took. His balls slapped violently, as she rotated her hips with his motion. Her legs stayed locked, so he could fuck as hard as he wanted to. Candice was enjoying the moment just not the person. Kofi's face was now between her ass cheeks. He spread them and spit on her anus. Then used the flat of his tongue to rustle back and forward. Candice cried out. Her body was reacting to all his moves. Seconds later, his penis pressed in the back of her throat. She gripped his ass with both hands and moved up and down his dick like a prostitute at work.

Gagging and slurping, Candice sucked until she felt his body going rigid. She released the hold with her mouth and teased the tip of his penis with her fingers. Kofi's body was frozen. He urged her to let him climax, but Candice denied the request. "Not now," she whispered. Candice squeezed his firmness and pulled it back, so the head would swell. She let saliva drip from her jaws as she looked into his eyes. "Please," Kofi said vulnerably.

"Come on, pick up!" Candice begged as she rested her back against a dirty brick wall. "Bastard!" She said frustratingly. At a time like this Melvin was nowhere to be found. Candice excluded Uber for fear of being placed in this area. Her whereabouts could not be involved. The line continued to ring in her ear. Even though her face was heavily wrapped, Candice still wanted nothing to do with this side of town.

"Hello Candi," a male voice replied.

Startled, she jumped. Candice took short deep breaths to calm herself. "Melvin why you wait so long to answer? I've been calling you for a while." She complained. The sound of a baritone voice, in the background told her the excuse before he said it. She exhaled in defeat. He giggled. "I have company mind you, so what's important? Stop will you Travis."

"I need you to come, get me and I'll explain once you're here." Candice whispered while looking out in the dark street.

"What!" Melvin exclaimed. "Leave this handsome man to be in the cold. I don't think so." Candice tone rose. "MELVIN! This is no playing matter...please." Reluctantly he agreed. "Tell me where you're at."

CHAPTER FIVE

MIKAL

His two-story house featured five fireplaces and an open floor plan that focused on the tropical landscape design surrounding. The trees on his land was trimmed precise to highlight the stone driveway, leading to his, four-car garage. Mikal looked over his property with pride. Hard work and dedication had him enjoying the fruits of his labor. This was the first morning since Secret Confessions dropped their album, that the paparazzi was not camped in front of his 7,450 sq. foot home. As much as he loved privacy, Mikal understood what came with his status. No doubt the stress was piling up, especially with the new pressure added by Kimberly Jones; the owner of Street Approved Records.

Mikal like the confidence she showed in him. That made the task easier. Questions already did, jumping jacks inside his head. In order, to go head to head with a diva like Rihanna, you had to possess those same qualities. It was a tricky situation but one he could accomplish. Whoever she was, her voice and looks had to demand attention. Plus, the woman had to have attitude that said she was here to stay. With those characteristics and achievements, it would be plentiful and with him on her side, they would go all the way up. No way would he allow himself to fail. *All the way!* Mikal told himself.

"Now if I fuck this model/and she just bleached her asshole/and get bleach on my T-shirt/I'm a feel like an asshole..."

Kanye West's latest hit blasted through the speakers of his home gym. Mikal listened close to the production. He admired everything about West. The man dared the world to contain his personality. Dared the world to control his imagination. Dared them to judge his progress. DARE! DARE! DARE! It explained why he was so open to experiencing the unexperienced. They both were Gemini's so Mikal understood him more then he cared to believe. There was still along way to go, in order, to reach Kanye's level but that's where he was reaching to go. His thoughts were interrupted by his best friend. "Nigga you done got scared of this iron?" It's yo' set."

Aubrey Jones was standing next to the weight bench with his chest sticking inches away from his body.

He was an exotic car salesman, who sold some of the most expensive whips to Hollywood's biggest stars. The Lambo, Bentley coupe, Range Rover and the Porsche sedan, were all thanks to him. A.J. was five foot six and thick. They had been friends since grade school and one of the people that helped him when things were shaky. Mikal had nothing but love for the man. "Come on nigga let's go!" A.J. said while patting his chest hard. "It's sittin' on 245. I wanna see how you eat that up."

The comment made Mikal laugh. '245 ain't shit playa, I eat that fo' breakfast." Sweat dripped from his face as he adjusted his hand against the bar. "You smilin' but it's real here. Count to fifteen cause that's where I'm stoppin'. Matter of fact turn that up, while I get my cut." Mikal ordered. A.J did as his friend said and rocked to the crazy lyrics controlling the air waves. "It goes down in the DMM/it go down in the DM/I seen yo' girl post a, BM/so I hit her in the DM/all eyes yea I see'em/yea this yo' man I hate to be him..." A.J yelled as he stumped around the room like a peacock. "Eat nigga! Eleven! Twelve! Thirteen! That's what I'm talkin' about! That's what I'm mu'fuckin' talkin' about!" Mikal locked his jaws tight as he replaced the weight back on the rack. That was the assault they handed to the stack for the next hour.

This was a weekly routine done at least four times. His partners company helped him relax and relieve some of the stress. A.J and Mikal lounged in his living room, talking. His partner was still wiping water from his ears after the hot shower taken. "Nigga you listenin' to me?" Mikal asked.

"Yea man!" A.J responded. "Some water stuck in my ear."

"It's good, somethin' back there."

A.J paused for a second to give Mikal a sarcastic look. "There we go. Now what you were sayin'?" Mikal leaned back in his sofa. "We got a party jumpin' off on the twenty-eighth of this month. It's gonna be a lot of stars there. Fo' sho' people like Rita Ora, Kourtney Kardashian, Kendall Jenner and Ciara just to name a few... but you know if it's hoes, there's niggas comin' to put a hoe in one," He laughed at his analogue.

This was the first time Mikal mentioned the party and it was showing on A.J face. He wasn't happy about the late invite. "Man why?"

Mikal raised his hand. "Don't go bitch on me nigga. I got too much on my plate. You gonna be there, if nobody else arrives. Here's what I need though. "He rubbed the flat of his hand over his waves to smooth them out. "As many bad chicks you know. How many can you get? Let me know. Not all of them comin' but I'ma' make you the playa of the year with this move."

A.J nodded but was still confused. "Explain this a little better, please. You know I'm special." Both men started laughing. "Aight, entertainment for men and women. Major niggas want bad bitches. Jigga, Yeezy, Jeezy, and Chris Breezy... gone be in the buildin'." Mikal said. "I'm lookin' fo' new talent so I have the opportunity to find it with this crowd."

A.J laughed in response. He understood the way Mikal thought. Having that many women, around that many stars, would separate the gold diggers from the boss chicks. If they were there to truly make a name for themselves, Mikal's intelligence would find them. If they weren't, then they would be a one-night stand. "Plus," Mikal added. "I'm tryin' to fuck something different. New clothes, new two doors and new hoes, is what this life is about."

His friend smiled. "Now seriously, what type of chick you lookin' for to compete against Rihanna. That bitch is untouchable, for the moment. She got niggas and bitches actin' silly behind her sexy ass." A.J chuckled, then shook his head.

Mikal stood and walked to his wet bar. "That's a good question A.J." He had not thought about that. The woman must have a certain type of charisma about herself. He knew that much. Two glasses of Italy produced tangerine flavored Moscato was in his hand, when he returned. A.J accepted one with no complaints. Morning had dwindled into noon so neither one of them was in a hurry to leave. They sipped quietly for a moment before the sweet beverage started to take effect.

"What do you think about Kim?" Mikal asked. Their minor incident had him itching to taste her.

"What kinda question is that?"

"One that needs an answer." Mikal stated.

A.J washed some drink around in his mouth and hunched his shoulders. "I wish I had a shot at that Nicki Minaj built thing. That's all I can say."

His words were all that needed to be said because Mikal was feelin' the same way. She was weighing heavy on his mind. He just had not figured out how to come at her without being disrespectful. Her position made things difficult and Mikal was aware of that. It was something about Kim that kept grabbing his attention away from reality. Mikal walked back to the marble counter and retrieve the whole bottle of Moscato, before seating himself again. "I wanna fuck her bro." He said abruptly. "You and a lot more niggas but who has she fucked with?" A.J asked.

Mikal nodded. Answering that was harder then it seemed. That's what excited him. All it took was good planning and he thought he was up for the job. "Check this out, fo' the record I'm gonna do it." Mikal said matter of fact. A.J wrinkled his face as the music played. The liquor had him in a party mood. Mikal let it roll awhile longer, then turned it off. "What you think?'

"That was live. Kinda like a mixture of Pop and R&B." A.J responded. Mikal raised and headed toward the back to get dressed. "That's just what I wanted to hear. The bitch I make a star has to match that beat because I produced that for Rihanna."

CHAPTER SIX

CANDICE

Melvin loaded the last of their luggage, in the rear of the minivan taxi and hopped in next to Candice. She wore a distinct look since the midnight incident and still nothing was revealed to him. Melvin didn't want to pry, but it bothered him a lot. She was his only friend. "To the airport, sir." He instructed the driver. Candice had secrets; who didn't. He had known that from day one of their meeting each other. This just added to what was already there. "Try to relax a while darling. It's a long flight ahead of us. As soon as we're checked in our hotel, you must tell me what's going on." Melvin crinkled his nose. "I've worked too hard with you to be shut out...you hear me?"

Now they sat side by side in first class, traveling to Dallas, Texas and Candice continued to be silent. Melvin pressed his back deeper into the thick cushion seat, trying to get comfortable. He opened his eyes for a second before reclosing them. The situation was starting to agitate him because she would not sleep. Their trip was at least seven hours long and Candice needed to rest. Melvin wanted to say something, but decided against it, fearing it would do no good. Instead, he took the time to prepare for what lies ahead of them. Luck was to thank for this trip because Ms. Jones, of Street Approved Records was all business like the industry mentioned. The treatment he received was something to remember. None of his phone calls was returned. Everyday Melvin tried a new tactic and all them resulted in nothing. Then an email with Candice Galvez's picture attached, the woman softened.

Reluctantly, Ms. Jones sent invitations. *Candi it's on you now!* Melvin thought. The doors were open, but the hard part was yet to come. As beautiful as she was, it would take more than that. Women in the same category would be all around. No doubt she was seductive and demanded attention. He'd seen her in action when she really wanted something. This was her life, her dream and for her to succeed, want, had to be at the top of the list. This was a once in a life time opportunity. He hoped she realized that herself.

They were two weeks earlier than planned. That was more time then needed, but do to the circumstance, accepted. The weather was slightly warmer than the East Coast and both wanted to enjoy it. "Where are you going Candi?" In this city there's men waiting to snatch you up. Not that you'd mind." Melvin rolled his eyes. "Mel I'm beginning to think you want me." Candice replied. A look of astonishment sat on his face. She laughed good naturally, before continuing. "I need to see what this city has to offer. After all, I might be relocating to Dallas." Candice winked. "Once I return, I'll fill you in on what happen like you asked."

Melvin said nothing. He was used to the up and down roller coaster ride she took him on. His friend Candice was a work in progress. Once she left, Melvin stretched across the bed and turned on the television. He flipped through the channels looking for something interesting. It was 3:00 pm and it surprised him, that Candi wanted to go out so quickly. Her mood changed as soon as they were away from the state of New York. Saying it was strange was an understatement. Melvin stopped on CNN world news when a familiar sight caught his attention. "At Terrace Garden Dr. Kofi Siriboe was found in his room dead on the tenth floor. There seems to be no signs of foul play, but the authorities are looking for the person that was with him, for questioning. Mr. Siriboe, known for some of his work on women like Kylie Jenner, Meagan Fox, had high levels of alcohol in his system."

"It's said he had allergy medication in his coat pocket but was unable to reach it. Though it's unsure how the large amount of peanut oil was used to prepare Dr. Siriboe food. Family and friends, we ask that you call…" The feeling of pain shot up his back and all of a, sudden Melvin felt nauseous. He pressed mute and begin pacing around the room. He didn't believe in coincidence. Candice either knew about the situation or had something to do with it. Everything made more sense. Her call. Her anxiousness to rid New York. Her paranoid state. It all made sense now. Melvin sat down hard in the sole chair of the hotel and pulled at his short cut blondish hair. She'd found a way to do it again. One time a year this woman brought turmoil to his doorsteps. Nothing was promised at that moment, he had to claim himself. "Candi you're a real bitch." Melvin spit.

If it was fact, as always, it was up to him to be damage control. He picked up the phone and dial home. "Travis hello sweetheart. NO! NO! NO! Everything's fine" Melvin listened, then started giggling. "Here's what I need of you. Honestly, I miss you too. After the ordeal, I should be back in your arms." He giggled again and replaced the receiver. Candice was a part of his life, so he had to protect her, even if she did not expect it. "You better have a good explanation." He filled his nose with a long line of cocaine and stripped down to sit in the hot tub. For the next five hours Melvin waited in the steaming heat.

Stars sprinkled across the sky by the time Candice came prancing through the door, followed by a bellhop and carrying a ton of Macy's bags. She was in a splendid mood and it could be heard in her voice. "Never meant to cause you pain/I just wanna go back, to being, the same and I/only wanna make things right/before you walk out my life…" Candice danced and sang Monica's old song. Noticing him, she quickly handed the man a tip and shut the door. "Melvin what's wrong with you and put some clothes on. You're not enticing me…at all."

Her agent, friend and closes consultant showed no signs of awareness. He rose from the bed and immediately she knew he was high. Melvin watched her as she removed the merchandise from her bags with no care in the world. His life was on the line and she didn't care. "Candi, we need to talk. I saw the news. Please tell me what's going on and please don't... lie." Melvin's words stumbled loose. Candice looked like a deer in headlights standing, in the middle of the room. That itself said volumes. "What happened Candi?" You know I'm always here for you...just be honest with me." Melvin said. Candice sat next to him, ignoring the fact that he was still naked. She placed her face in her hands and begin to cry. "Where do I begin? It's..." Sniffs. "So much you don't know. Promise me it won't leave this room." Melvin embraced her. "I promise Candi." It starts at the time of my mother's death."

CHAPTER SEVEN

MIKAL

What I need from you is understandin'/how can we communicate/if you don't hear what I say/what I need from you is understandin'/so simple as one, two, three..."

Escape's 1990's hit single blast through his speakers, as he raced around the turn of 635, heading toward far north Dallas. Mikal like revisiting old songs to help him create something with unique substance. Many of the earlier productions was done precise and those sounds tended to stand the test of time. He pressed into his gas pedal, to add turbulence to the engine. The speedometer moved toward 100 miles per hour. Mikal bounced along to the wood grain steering wheel tightly, while he glanced to both sides of the freeway, for any hidden Dallas police cars.

It was good he saw none. Dealing with them wasn't on his most wanted list. For the last year, since purchasing this black on black Lamborghini, he'd gotten tickets twice a month. That 200 on dash, combined with the V12 seemed to much not to reach for. He laughed openly and rearranged his Michael Kors frames on his face. Mikal caught a glimpse of his reflection off the passage side window. *Michael Kors shirt, Burberry tie and David Hart suit!* The look enhanced his 230-pound body, showing more shapes then a tenth-grade geometry class. He wanted just that for the engagement, ahead. All the members of Secret Confessions would be present, as well as Kim and Tracy McDavis. His surprise visits to see his nephew gave Kim the idea. Timing was everything.

Mikal admitted she was on her game. Secret Confessions to 40,000 copies in the last month so what better time than now. If that didn't make a good impression, nothing would. In addition, Mikal wanted to meet the man behind all the record label stories. He exited Greenville Ave. and turned into the parking lot of his female friend's restaurant. First take eatery was owned by Priyanka Alexander was a former beauty pageant, with Indian nationalities. That gave her the edge in different dishes she served at her place. Mikal and her, were friends and through that they started dating but like so many of his relationships, it failed. The only thing separating her from the rest she kept in contact. One call and reservations were made.

He adjusted his suit coat and stepped into the cool morning. His wrist was complimented with a diamond bracelet and Rolex watch. Mikal grabbed the Giorgio Armani Private handbag and strolled toward the entrance way. Everyone was seated with menu's in their hands, when he approached the table. Tracy was the first to stand and greet him. "Glad you can make it baby. I've heard a lot about you. This is my boy Shun." Shun raised and duplicated the gesture. Both men were about his weight and height. From the looks of their surroundings, nobody was disappointed at what they saw. Smiles were kidnapping all the woman's faces. Moni was next to stand and embrace him, followed by Pam and then Rachel.

"It's nice y'all in a good mood." Mikal said. He resumed standing, looking over the group. "Why wouldn't we be. I'm blessed....and you're a blessin'." Tracy said. "I want my brother's label to keep doin' what it does." That made Mikal smile. Kim raised up and pulled out a chair next to her. "Take a seat handsome. I took the liberation to order you something. Hopefully you not to picky." She winked at him. If a man of his hue could blush; she'd succeeded in accomplishing that. Mikal did a quick in-take of his peers. Everyone was business with one another except Moni. She stared at him every chance given. Moni wanted him. It was written all over her. He decided to try something. It would be risky but fun. Removing his phone, Mikal texted her. *Restroom 20 min!* "Scuse me fo' that." He replaced the phone back in his bag and winked at Moni.

Moni laughed as she read her screen. "Is anyone else going to make some calls before I start talking?" Kim asked. "Well then, right now we're at the top of the hit chart...again and I'd like for it to stay that way. With the help of Mikal, I think we're at the top of the chart...again and I'd like for it to stay that way. With the help of Mikal, I think we're in good shape. At the party I want new talent, so everyone can keep their eyes open for that special person." She paused to let her words set in. "Mikal it's on you." Kim touched his hand gently.

Shortly after their meals arrived, Moni left the table. Mikal followed five minutes later. When he hit the corner, he gave a silent prayer for the single restroom format. That part was confusing him. Mikal stepped inside and leaned his back against the door. "There's not much time." Moni whispered. As she tore at his belt buckle. Instantly, he was erect. Moni freed him and massaged him quickly. "Damit Moni!" Her lips were wrapped around his nine inches, sucking repeatedly. She lifted his balls and masterfully gulped most of his dick down her throat. Her hot mouth made him orgasm faster than he thought possible. Mikal gripped the back of her head and bit into his lips. "OOOH SHIT!" Moni didn't fight him. She swallowed all his seeds until there was no more, never loosing eye contact. His green eyes had her in a trans.

Kim studied him when he returned. The look in her eyes said more than he cared to admit. "Was everything O.K.?"

Mikal forged a frown. "What's that mean?"

"A question with a question, huh?" She shook her head. "Those eyes are going to get you into something you just might like." Heat rose around him from the constant stares. Moni's face was red. Promptly, Mikal accommodated to the situation. He could not let her intimidate him. "Boss," he said audaciously. "...don't end up my wife." The people around snickered. Tracy grabbed his glass of juice. "Yea, Kim I like him."

Energy raced through his veins like the horsepower running through the engine, he controlled. His mind was on Kimberly Jones. The way her short but thick structure pushed against the one-piece pantsuit. He couldn't remove that sight from his mind. Her bare skin and it's Chanel coating, had him on the verge of craziness. Mikal smashed down harder into the gas petal. It always helped him to speed, like they say, it ain't what you think it is, look around. Kim's attraction we're more than physical. She shared his overall vision for the future. Less important matters took a backseat ride to changing the game ahead. Mikal thought about what he'd read: Docility and submission especially from a strong black woman is not a sign of weakness. It is in fact the highest form of trust, respect, adoration and gratitude for her king.

To have a woman that was willing to give that was what he wanted. Kim was the woman who would give that to the right man. Mikal just didn't know how to get her to see him differently. What he wanted he always got. She was on the radar. "Shit!" Mikal exclaimed. Not

Paying attention had gotten him in trouble again. A set of red and blue flashers was behind his car. Kim in the blind was already causing problems. That made things more enticing. He could do nothing but laugh as he pulled over.

CHAPTER EIGHT

CANDICE

For the past three days, Candice was cooped in her hotel room fantasying about the brief encounter with Mikal Edwards. Melvin knew all the spots that the hometown celebrities of Dallas, visited. Everyday with him was exhilarating. On many occasions, she became overwhelmed with the picture she saw but nothing compared to Wednesday interaction. Even though, fame was something she frequently administered, Candice couldn't control the excitement of being so close to all of them. "This better not be how you react at the party." Melvin said. "Or we're screwed." His words teased her mind, as she lay across the bed. Those eyes on a man that dark, stunned her. She wasn't sure, but it was possible that he spoke French to someone passing by.

Candice grabbed the pillow, stuffed its softness to her face, and squeezed her legs tightly together. Mikal was more handsome, in person, than any magazine display. Fifty Shades of Grey kept running its scenes through her head. It was silly because he barely gave noticed to her as he entered the ladies' restroom behind one of Secret Confessions members. Candice giggled. Not only was he God's gift to women but daring too. He smiled when he saw she knew what was going on. Candice understood those spontaneous setting and the excitement it brought. She rolled to her side because the feeling was taking toll on her. The way his tall frame drowned out her petite figure, made it seem like a giant was walking through.

His bold fragrance consumed her nose. *Mr. Burberry!* His smoothness dominated every step. His dark complexion, all coexisted with each other. *Damit!* He was an A-plus without trying. Handsome and famous was a dangerous combination. Candice thought about the name stationed around him...Kimberly Jones, NBA star Tracy McDavis, Secret Confessions, and Priyanka Alexander. That said volumes, when the owner tended you, instead of allowing her entourage the opportunity. She sat up, rustled her hair, and walked to the mirror in their hotel room. Perfection stared back. Firm breast, flat stomach, and sculpted legs challenged men at every gathering she attended. With so many elite women, Candice feared being unable to separate herself from the rest.

The hardest part of life regress so what was needed to overcome that? Candice looked over her shoulder as she thought about the question. What man would not want her? "One that has many just like you." She answered frankly. "What? Who are you talking to?" Melvin raised to one elbow and wiped at his eyes. In her train of thought, she'd totally forgotten about his presence. "Nothing Mel. Get some sleep. There's many more places to visit... and your disturbing my thinking."

He pulled the covers over his head. "Try doing it quietly, will you?" She smirked as she closed the door and stepped in the shower. It was early in the morning and the day was still ahead of them. Things had to be prepared because this was her one shot. This wasn't a photoshop. It was all or nothing. Candice let the hot water run down her body. She relaxed and ran her fingers through her hair. One week from today was the main-focus. Her future would be determined by the performance exhibited at that party.

Candice shut the faucet off and stepped onto the tile floor. A thought came to the forefront of her mind, that could give her the edge needed against her opponents. His brief personality peek gave her a beginning map about who he was. She knew what needed to be done. Candice had a model friend that was attending the party also, Taylor Rimes. The woman knew more about celebrities, then anyone should be authorized. People said she was the next Wendy Williams, but most of her gossip was facts. Candice walked in the room, letting the air dry her skin. She sat down, grabbed her phone and dialed. "Hello sorry for the early morning call but I really need your help. Do you know Mikal Edwards? Yes, Yes, That's him. Can you tell what you know about him?" Candice listened. "Well because it's you, I'm planning to be a singer and I hear he's the best in the business."

She hung up, knowing half of the state of New York would have the information before tomorrow. That was alright because by the time it made it back this way the damage would be done.

CHAPTER NINE

MIKAL

"Come on baby! You sittin' over there half dressed, lookin' crazy. It's the hottest night of the year." A.J. said as he arranged his Versace designer shirt. His attitude was turnt up because everything that lies ahead. No way would that depressed mindset hinder him from enjoying this night. "Hey playa, all these hoes, in stilettos, with unlimited amount, of pesos." He chuckled. "How you ain't amped?" Mikal smirked at his friend. It was hard to make him understand what he was up against. No one set goals higher then him and this was no different than the rest. "That's because I have to pick from all these hoes, with no pesos." The reference made them laugh.

"Well, there's a bunch to choose from." A.J. added his diamond cuff links. "I used all of those invitations. What you think...Red Bottom to give me some hip hop flava or straight loafers?" A wave of the hand was the answer A.J. received, when Mikal left the room.

STREET APPROVED HOLIDAY BASH

December 28, 2016 was one of the most legendary events of Dallas, Texas history. Fashion and celebrities pushed the limit like a fat man in some spandex pants. Even though, the entrance way was marble, everyone walked across it like it was Hollywood's Red Carpet, display. Champagne bottles and single roses complimented the tables for people to relax. Music demolished the ears of everyone present in the ballroom. Street Approved graffiti welcomed visitors as they danced on the floor. Showing on the big screen was a picture of a black panther wearing a white cocktail suit, with the inscription: TAKIN' OVA THE GAME! From the sales of records, that couldn't be denied. There only competition, Drake and Rihanna.

After tonight, Mikal planned to erase their challenge and that wouldn't be easy. Especially with ROC Nation in the mix. Jigga man had forgotten more about business, than his years of living, but if you're shooting to become the best, try the best. Tracy and Kim approached him looking spectacular. Mikal nursed a glass of pink Cîroc cherry fruit mixed, while leaning on the bartender counters. Tracy wore a tan Dolce & Gabbana suit, but Kim's strapless Prada gown and stilettos caught his eyes. *Electrifying!* He acknowledges both. "How does it feel to steal the show?" People were walking up to Tracy effortlessly.

Tracy laughed. "This is yo' world. One night of fun fo' me and I'm back to Miami. It's all about you." Tracy looked around. "I see a lot of bad mamas in here though."

Kim made a coughing sound. "Anyone notice me standing here?" Grins but no responses. She faked a frown.

"You're a part of that comment." Mikal intervened.

Her lips transformed into a smile. "You're to smooth. Honestly, there's a bunch of females in here. What did you do, open the doors to Dallas?"

"No, but this atmosphere will allow me to see what I'm workin' with. A.J. is the playa, playa." Mikal chuckled as he locked eyes with an, Hispanic hottie. Her style, with the red Gucci thigh-high dress embracing her curvy figure, was a potential star showdown to any of the top names in the building. "You know that nigga a trick. Where he at anyhow?" They searched the party momentarily. "I think he in that direction." Shun pointed behind him. "Where Penelope Cruz and Selena Gomez, was sittin'" He approached the crowd.

"Let me head that way befo' this nigga fuck something up." Mikal dapped the fellas and embraced Kim longer than necessary. Her soft body and powerful perfume were mind blowing. He was amazed at the star power in the building. During his brief stroll across the room, celebrities like Janelle Monae, John Legend and couple, Bella and The Weekend, could be seen. That made him relax some. This was by far the place to be.

A.J. was nowhere to be found as he continued to tour the Dallas Ballroom Lounge. Glasses were filled, the music was good, and the dance floor packed just like he'd planned. Celebrities were normal people that loved to chill and enjoy themselves but at an expensive price. Mikal played the good host like boss lady wanted, huh here, hand shake there. A tap on the shoulder had drawn, his attention. Standing in front of him was the hot Hispanic woman, he'd seen earlier. She was more attractive then Mikal thought. "Mikal Edwards, right?" Candice asked matter of fact.

He said nothing, choosing silence as he continued to study her. The woman's features were beautiful, and she stood there confident. Her size was the mirror image of Rihanna, it was competition, but what accessories didn't she not have. "Can I help? You're havin' a good time, right?"

Candice gave an off-handed smile. 'It's one of the best parties I've attended in some time." She looked away. His piercing green eyes was hard to maintain eye contact with.

Once Candice gathered herself, she continued. "I was hoping to have a picture with you...something to add to my memoir." She wanted to tread lightly with him. At that moment, the person he was looking for appeared. "Just in time. Here." Mikal handed the woman's phone to A.J. "Take some pictures fo' us." Candice eased into his arms, resting his arms around her waist. It surprised him how comfortable she was with the whole ordeal. Several photos later, they parted ways. "Thank you." Candice said as she slowly sashayed her hips with each step. A.J. showed all his teeth while watching. "Damn that bitch bad. I see you ain't missin' a beat. That's yo' choice?"

Mikal shook his head. "No...she fit the category though. Everything is there. I was thinkin' the same thing because she could challenge the industry. I have to be careful. I don't want a Rita Ora...some type of pop one hit wonder, feel me?'

A.J stood there saying nothing. His eyes franticly scanned back and forth along each table. Excitement was being siphon out his pores. "Your cool playa? Don't pass out in here cause I ain't givin' you no mouth to mouth reciprocation. Yo' ass gonna be out of there." Mikal touched his shoulder to calm him down. "I need yo' help baby."

A.J. downed his cup of Rose', to calm his nerves. "I'm Gucci. What's up?"

"I have to make some moves, get that chick info fo' me. Her soft ass body made me fo'get to ask her name. Damn, she given these stars a run fo' their money." Mikal watched another woman, who resembled Dascha Polanco. This gonna be hard!" He told himself. Nobody comes unprepared" ...and find me one more. The top five tonight is what I'm choosin' from." Mikal left without another word.

CHAPTER TEN

STREET APPROVED RECORDS CALLED!
Apprehensively, Candice paced in circles, wearing only lace panties and a bra. Her ear was pressed to the receiver of her cell phone, listening intently to the caller. Three weeks passed since the party and the producer showed no signs of interests, but here she was with an early morning call. The encouraging talks given by Melvin didn't seem to work. Daily she waited for a call. How could her reality be left in someone else's hands? Life was so cruel! "Yes, I'll hold." Candice placed her hand over the receiver. "They're connecting me to his office." She couldn't hold back the excitement she was feeling. "We have to find a condo." Melvin rolled his eyes and continued to bounce his feet.

The response agitated her so much, Candice gave him the bird. That jarred laughter from Melvin. "Hello Ms. Candice Galvez."

"Yes, this is her." She placed a finger to her lips, silencing anything further.

"Sorry fo' not contactin' you faster, but the holidays can be hectic." Mikal said.

"You're absolutely right." Kem could be heard playing in the background. That combined with baritone voice had her fantasizing what could be, even at this moment. "I've interviewed three women prior to contactin' you and neither of them impressed me." Mikal let his words nail themselves in her head for a second. "Candice to be straight with you so I don't waste your time and vise versa, can you sing or are you just shootin' blanks, hopin' to hit?"

She stopped and took several breaths to calm herself. It was about to happen. The wrong answer could send the wheels churning in the opposite direction than she desired. "Hello Ms. Galvez." Mikal said. Candice had totally lost track that her life was on the line. "I'm sorry…I went into little girl syndrome. I…, I'm just so overwhelmed. I don't mean to act this way but wow…your friend explained to me, but never in a million years did I …sorry, sorry, to answer your question, yes."

Mikal couldn't hold back his laughter. "The man you're speakin' of is A.J. he told me something about you being able to dance and model. Is that true?"

Candice gathered her composure. "Yes. I have tapes of both. Would you like for me to send them?"

"No, but you can bring them with you, when you come for an interview." Mikal said. "I'm different from other producers. I like to hear you under some of my productions. Do you have time?"

Do I have time! Candice wanted to yell. I have time nothing but time! Instead she said, "Of course, when would you like to meet?"

"February 9th, that's a Tuesday at 10 o'clock. How's that sound?"

"Tuesday February 9th, that's a date." Candice looked at Melvin who was jotting everything down. "Thank you, Mr. Edwards. I won't disappoint you."

"Please Mikal."

Candice smiled. "In that case, Candi."

He laughed slightly before disconnecting. Candice ran and dove into bed, giggling and kicking at the air.

"Mel, we did it! We did it!"

Melvin stood and looked at the time. The clock on the stand read: 11:30 a.m. "Well it's more to be done. You got a call and I'm sure that he hasn't signed you yet. What did handsome say?"

Candice went through every detail pertaining to their conversation just returning to the small encounter made her feel like Drake: Controlla. "Candi you may be on to something darling. I'll be back later."

"Where are you going at a time like this?"

Melvin slipped on his jacket. "I'm tired of this hotel room. Plus, we need a condo and a car. You're about to be a star.

TUESDAY FEBRUARY 9, 2017

Mentally, the day of the meeting took longer than the actual time frame. Time seemed to slow all the way down. From dust to dawn, she walked around practicing her vocals. Not that her personal lesson would attain anything, but it made her feel good. On a few occasions, dance moves were implemented into the rehearsals. This was Candice's form of therapy used in stressful situations, like now. With all that done, she was still nervous. Who wouldn't be? Riding in the back of the label's limousine, she overlooked her gear. Pink halter top, tight fitting denim jeans equipped with holes in the knees and high-rise black boots top off her attire. Most men enjoyed seeing a woman sexy and classy.

Candice adjusted her Chanel sunglasses while looking at Melvin, next to her. He was crouched over shoving white powder, up his nose. The sight made her shiver. His drug dependency was becoming heavier each day. Sometimes she wondered how long would to take to destroy their friendship? As of now, that hadn't happened. Luckily, the problem was in the dark. She understood what he'd done for her brand, but the question was could he keep doing it going forward. Watching him, Candice was curious about that.

"Mel." Candice whispered, not wanting the driver to hear their conversation. "Mel…will you stop already?

We're five minutes out and that's your second time powdering your nose." Melvin looked at her. His eyes red and snorting nonstop. He removed the Clear eye from his top coat pocket.

After carefully applying, he spoke. "Sometimes you worry too much. I've kept your career relevant. Now your uncomfortable with- "Melvin brushed his nose with the back of his hand. "As long as you succeed, don't worry about me."

"But- ",

He waved his hands, "No buts...don't worry. I'm all business." Candice focused on the passing cars outside her window. Even though, she didn't like it, she let it be. This wasn't the time to be at each other's throat. Candice made a mental note to revisit this conversation later.

CHAPTER ELEVEN

MIKAL

Mikal sat behind his desk, reading one of his favorite urban authors, Derrick Johnson's latest release: Pimpin' Is A Must. The dude was one of his old friends that had a bad turn in life, sending him to prison, but continued to strive in his writing. He'd asked if Mikal could read the book and help him promote. So far, the context was something he liked. Most people spent their whole life judging the way someone else should live, when they can't even grasp which way their driving. Life has many different stages and society liked to overlook that aspect. They think everyone will become lawyers, doctors, and movie stars, but the reality of the situation, was people venture in areas. Many become prostitutes, dope fiends and much more. Our judgmental state doesn't change that.

The only change relies on the individual that's stuck in that situation. If you want something you never had, do something you've never done. His intercom beeped, causing him to set aside his book. "Mr. Edwards."

"Yes," He responded.

"Candice Galvez and her agent Melvin Cannon is here to see you."

Mikal looked at his watch. They were right on time. "Aight send them up."

Her agent entered first, followed by Candice. Mikal gave a silent approval at what he saw. The floor length trench coat brought attention to the rest of her clothing. Trophy she was. He stood and shook each person's hand. "Glad y'all could come. Candi, right?"

Him remembering her nickname brought a smile that showed perfect teeth. Mikal pointed toward the chairs, then continued. "There's a possible contract on the table. That's my reason fo' havin' you here today. Your performance is what's goin' to determine that. I'm behind the eight ball right now so you have that on your side. This is unusual because I don't know anything about you except that your beautiful." He winked. "That's undeniable, but it takes more than that to make a big splash in the game, feel me? From all interviews that I've done, you're the one that stuck out most...it's like you were primped fo' this shit."

Mikal steepled his fingers behind his head. Melvin took that opportunity to speak. "Here is the video with all the work she'd been involved in. Candi has graced the cover of Latina magazine and did some commercials for Cover Girl. Not only is she stunning, but she brilliant too!"

Mikal grabbed the disk and immediately pushed it in the DVD player next to his desk. "What makes her so brilliant?" He asked.

"Well Candi has—"

Candice interrupted him. "Mel please. I'm a four-year graduate in fashion designing. I started modeling because a friend saw me and wanted to photograph me. The word spread and that was that. I'm here because I'm trying to take my career to the next level. If that will help?"

Nodding his head, Mikal continued to watch the screen. Candice was intriguing. Nothing on this set was photoshopped. In his life, he only seen natural twice and from what he was watching, Candice was becoming the third. He let the tape play. The rose peddled tattooed against her body caught his attention. What else could she add to her beauty. Mikal prayed he'd hit the jackpot.

Hopefully, Rihanna had a challenger. He begins smiling and he faced them. "I'll introduce you to the owner and CEO of this label once we complete our studio test. That will show me where we stand. I plan on signin' you today, but that's on you." Mikal asked. "Are you ready?"

"Yes, I think so."

"Aight here's some old lyrics from Alicia Keys…just tryin' to find your voice type. Lookin' at you, I think that's about where you are, but…" Mikal shrugged his large shoulders.

"We'll see. Then we move on to the real test." He leads them down the hall to their studio.

If liquor take control of you, it had taken total ownership of him. Long ago Mikal had switched from drinking out of a glass to sipping straight from the bottle. Rihanna's video was playing on his flat screen against the wall. He studied her moves and watched the way she danced, the way she charmed the crowd, the way her tattoos outlined her body. Nothing went unscoped. Since contact with Candice, he'd become overly obsessed with RiRi. Her sexiness was maximized in each step she took. Mikal leaned back in the Jacuzzi and listened to Rihanna sing. An empty bottle sat next to a half-filled Cîroc container. Candice breast in her top looked like a wardrobe malfunction waiting to happen. That made him raise up, grab the bottle, and take a gulp. Why she was on his mind, he couldn't answer.

Gently, he rubbed his crotch area under the water, trying to calm his erect penis. Mikal needed some company because he couldn't stop thinking about the way she stood in the sound booth. "*Wow!* She was better then he'd expected. Her voice was nice, and any enhancements could come through production. Candice was a blessing to the label like Dak Prescott was to the Dallas Cowboys. The Cîroc was driving him right now while his thoughts sparked pictures of Kim, as she stood close to him in her office. Mikal lifted himself out the Jacuzzi and stumbled toward the living room. He wanted Kim, but something was drawing him to Candice. "Business first." Mikal said out loud. Sex was stirring up drama in his Group Secret Confessions.

Too much was riding on this to allow that to happen. Candice would take them by storm with heavy advertising and several billboards with her face. How could they duck that? He smiled at what the sign would read: TAKIN' OVA THE GAME! Kim agreed that she was the right person. Mikal picked up his phone and dialed Kim's number. "Hello," was the last words he remembered before passing out on the floor. "Hello, Hello...Mikal." Candice said in a sleepy tone.

CHAPTER TWELVE

CANDICE

Frightening screams traveled through the old wooden house. "STOP! PLEASE STOP! GOD HELP ME! NOOO PLEASE!" Rosie's voice bounced off the walls like a trampoline under children playing. Whichever word was said, made no difference because each syllable, fell on deaf ears. His punches continued to rain down on her. She lay balled up in the corner, inches away from unconsciousness. Jualian stepped back breathing heavily, holding a thick bottle of tequila, in his hand. It scared her. He carried no resemblance of the handsome man he once was. The sight was saddening. "Get up bitch." Rosie didn't raise; instead, she stole a quick glance around the room. A set of eyes watched from the crack of the doorway, face wet from the tears streaming down and fear painted the emotions for his mother.

She had to fight back. If not for herself, then for her children. "I said get up!" Her husband yelled. His beating was becoming more and more aggressive with every sip taken. Death would be the reality of the situation, if she didn't find away. What Rosie feared most was something happening to her child. One was already lost and that was the excuse Jualian was using to fuel his drinking. He blamed her for what transpired. Slowly she rose from the floor with blood dripping from her lip. The dark stain near her feet, made the filthy carpet, look even more nasty. He smiled slyly. "What!" Jualian spread his arms demurely. "Here, I know you want to kill me. Go 'head." Rosie didn't move. How could she? He was blocking her path and her body was aching from the beating she'd just endured. Their piercing stares was still there, looking, waiting and hoping. She inhaled, trying to give herself encouragement, and slowly stepped in his direction, but the unthinkable happened...

Candice woke from her dream cold, shivering and soaking wet from sweat. Her heart was punching against her chest like a caged bird, wanting freedom. Those dreams were starting to return. For years, she'd stayed stress free and all the bad memories had subsided, but now they were back. Back and making her relive the hatred that once was. Candice lay there until she was completely calm. Faintly voice could be heard coming from the lower half on her new Richardson condo. One foot at a time, she stood and walked into the bathroom. Her eyes were red and swollen from the rough night's sleep. Candice tended to herself before going down stairs, wrapped in a silk rob.

Shock registered in her face, when she reached the end of the stairs. Candice said nothing. The sight of them was conquering her mind. Melvin sat talking to Ebonie Johnson, in her living room. *What the fuck is she doing here!* Melvin was first to feel her presence. Good morning Candi, even though it's nearing 3 o'clock, Ms. Johnson flew down here late last night. She has some important information to share with you. I'm sorry this is such a surprise, but it totally slipped my mind."

Candice noticed white substance on her glass table, when she approached. Ebonie and her was not friends, no more than the devil and god. She eased in her love seat and folded her legs beneath her. "How long you two known each other. I'm not sure I understand what's going on."

Giggles erupted in the room. The drugs were probably more to blame than anything else. "Well, recently...Ms. Johnson contacted me about a month ago and now you say something." Candice yelled.

Melvin eyebrows raised. "It's not important. What's important is she thinks she can help." Candice looked at

89

the woman who was clenching her purse tightly in her lap. She was beautiful as a freshly polished china set. Her thick black wool coat with fur lining exposed the white pantsuit and snow boots. Elegance with a touch of bitch was all there. "Candice I'm not here to spoil your accomplishments," Ebonie begin. "I just have a few questions that's bothering me about Dr. Siriboe's death."

That puzzled Candice. "Why fly from New York, when you could get the same answer over the phone." Ebonie must've read her mind because she spoke. "It's the talk of the town. Many people knew allergies and it's not sitting right the way he died."

Candice frowned. "What are you asking?" She cut her eyes at Melvin. Their friendship was becoming a burden fast. Since the signing with the label, he had become unpredictable. "Am I a suspect because I wasn't notified?" Candice asked. Ebonie shook her head. "No but I had to talk to you...myself."

Melvin chimed in. "It's alright Candi."

"I can't believe you," Candice mouth sat gaped open. "Melvin what the fuck is wrong with you?"

Again, he started giggling. Nothing about this situation seemed funny to her. "can you please leave my house and don't return." Candice walked back toward the stairs as she watched her agent whispering, then nods of agreement were exchanged. Something had to be done. They could not be allowed to ruin what was going on. The one person she thought was on her side, now was the main cancer. His drug addiction was causing him to think irrationally. When a disease starts to infect the body, the only way to cure the problem was to remove it all together. Candice knew what had to be done.

She stood in the sound booth, with eyes closed and singing. Music was coming through her headphones clear. Mikal was on the other side of the glass listening. Everything he'd promise was standing true. Months of television shows, local and non-local radio stations and numerous billboards with her picture gracing each one. Slowly, she was beginning to gain followers. Her first single was in heavy rotation and the album wasn't done yet. Now Candice was recording the second, which was a woman empowerment song they reflected the sound of Mary J. Blige. "I gave up everything for you/understood what you wanted to do/and opened my heart to all your moves/but now I'm leaving you..."

Mikal stopped the music and lit the area. He was sitting comfortable behind the sound system. She loved his smooth demeaner. "Is there something wrong Candi?" Her words sputtered as she spoke. "No...um why you ask that?"

His icy teeth show with the next statement. "I know I've been workin' you a little hard so some of this may be my problem but today you're just not soundin' good. Notes off, face frownin'. You know, the feelin'. Mikal hunched his shoulders. Let's do it again...I'm sorry." Candice responded. He nodded his acceptance. "Are you sure nothin's wrong? I want to be more than your producer. We have to click on all cylinders like Timberland and crew." Mikal said. "I'm here ma."

When she started crying, Candice couldn't remember. All she knew was he was next to her, holding her against his chest and softly running his fingers through her hair. She continued to cry. The smell of his Issy Miyake overpowered the situation. Candice pulled away and wiped her eyes, trying not to smear her liner.

"I'm sorry. I don't know what came over me."

"That's aight. We'll continue tomorrow. It's fun," Mikal pointed at the plagues on the wall," but it'll be hell too. Would you like to come to lunch with me and we can finish this conversation?"

How could she refuse those eyes? "Sure, and I Promise not to cry again."

Mikal grinned as he reaches for his coat.

CHAPTER THIRTEEN

MIKAL

"What brought you to Dallas?" Mikal reasoned with himself, whether she would tell the truth. Her sexy facial expressions were clouding his rational thinking. Understanding that was impossible for him to realize right now. Her vanilla skin engulfed by his chocolate flesh had him drifting on a memory. That song was moving slow through his head, as he watched the moonlight emphasize the light perspiration, covering their body. Mikal's black satin sheets rested in the middle of her back, making the situation seem more than it really was, just sex! Excitement, supremacy, and submission captivated him every time he laid between her legs. He loved her in a way that would never be. No, matter when she called, his door opened.

Mikal couldn't help but think of Drake's verse. *I'm too good to you!* She toyed around with his abs awhile before answering. "I had some business to look into...nothing serious. You're not happy to see me?" She momentarily glanced in his eyes; then kissed his chest. "It's been over a year since we've been together."

"That's what's shockin'. Out of nowhere you call. Atlanta was out, last time we were together." Mikal pulled her on top of him, so he could look at her face. The low-cut hair style was a blessing and added to the sight of her cantaloupe size breast. He knew she wanted more because her nipples were erect, ready to be sucked. Mikal squeezed her waist. "Am I yo' playmate?"

She kissed him and pressed her body against his. "It's not like that. You knew the situation before we started." He did. "My husband is getting curious about these involuntary flights. I had to chill." She slid down his skin like a snake in the water. "You're still as big as the first day we met." Her small hands squeezed his huge penis causing the mushroom head to swell. Mikal didn't want anything serious at the time, but he was glad they'd exchanged numbers at the concert. High price pussy was always fun, but she became a fetish. That made him laugh.

"What's so funny?" Her body kneeled between his legs, slowly caressing him. Veins exploded through his skin, every time she motioned up and down. He bit into his lip, before closing his eyes. "How that feel?" She stroked him faster. A hot wet sensation made him gasp. "How do I let you control me?" The question was rhetorical. Her motion became intense and aggressive. She was sucking him like a savage. Then she stopped. "What, did you just get tender? I can get that at home. Fuck my face Mikal...make me want to leave him." With both hands, he grabbed her head and began pushing deep into her throat. Eyes watering, gagging and still slurping she endured the punishment. This was the reason he couldn't let go. She was a beautiful fucking freak with no need of his money.

When Mikal woke the next morning, he laid in his bed alone. Just like a thief in the night, she'd crept in his bed and stole his loving. He looked over to his ceiling fan and sang. "I wanna' spread the news/that if it feels this good getting used/girl just keep on using me/'til you use me up." Mikal started laughing uncontrollably. "What kind of playa are you?" He questions himself on the way to the shower. Early this morning, in the middle of the week, it had to be something jumping. If not, this was time to create because he was slipping. With this situation, he wasn't in the driver seat anymore.

"I used to think you was the playa of all time...nigga you trash." A.J said, as he sat behind his desk. "You ain't fucked that Puerto Rican hoe yet. I've been waitin', so I can hear how that pussy feel." He smiled.

"I remember a time you would've still had pussy juice on your boxer shorts." Mikal rubbed his wavy hair, then gave him the finger. "She cool daddy. I started to, but I gotta' make sure I don't fuck this up. Kim will kill me." A.J responded. "Now you don't know what you're doin'? You fuckin' them hoes in Secret Confessions and they ain't broke up." He shrugged his shoulders.

"Listen. I think I called her by accident,"

"By accident, nigga please." A.J gave him a smirk.

"Shut up and listen sometimes, I hate I came up here." Mikal looked in the lobby through the glass window.

"I was drunk my nigga...horny as hell. Shit I was like fuck it. I thought I called Kim. I was gonna' shoot my shot." He leaped from his seat resembling a basketball player.

His friend laughed. Mikal continued. "I think I called the wrong number. Candi asked me about it, but we left it at that."

"How did that conversation come up?" A.J was hungry to know everything. So, Mikal retold the story of her breakdown and dinner. A.J smiled. "What you think about that?"

"I don't know. Every woman I bump into got issues."

"Hell, nigga you got issues." A.J said.

Mikal stood up. His body was covered in Sean John gear. "Fuck off! I'm gone. I got some more shit to get into. Sittin' here ain't gonna' get it done because yo' weak ass addin' to the stress. Holla when you get off and when y'all supposed to get that new Maybach in?"

"Next week and you still scared of that hoe." A.J followed Mikal outside in the cool air. He got in his white Bentley and waved him off. He was to smart to get caught in that challenge.

"I got two phones/one fo' the plug and one fo' the load/I got two phones/one fo' the bitches and one fo' the doe/ Think I need two mo'/lab bumpin'. I'm ring, ring, ring/countin' money why ring, ring, ring/trap jumpin'/I'm ring, ring, ring..."

An hour of driving and jumping Kevin Gates, lead him to this big red brick house. Why he was here, was beyond Mikal's understanding. All he could remember was this is where his car stopped. His fingers drummed over the wood grain dash, as he watched the curtains move back and forth. They were looking at him like he was looking at them. The door open and the small frame of his mother appeared. Sabrina Edwards placed her hands on her hips and he could see she was smiling. It was an encouraging site. She waved him in. Mikal placed his head on the steering wheel. She wasn't the problem. Her heart wouldn't blame the man she loved so dearly. That was the reason he'd stop speaking to them both.

Finally, Mikal forced himself out of his ride and walked towards the house. This moment was well over due. When he entered, his father's features grabbed his attention. Mainly because his beard and hair were outlined in gray. That made him look older than fifty plus years. Carl Edwards relaxed in his plush Lazy Boy chair, reading a newspaper. "Glad you came in son." He never looked up.

"Yea, it's overdue." Mikal responded and took a seat across from him. His mother exited the kitchen carrying glasses of iced tea. After handing them out, she sat next to him and pulled his hand close kissing them tenderly. "I miss you baby." He could see her fighting back the tears. Sabrina was the true essence of a strong black woman and that was from the skin tone to deep in her heart.

She was the centerfold of knowledge, wisdom and understanding. A divine Queen for a true King. Mikal cuffed her tiny face. "I needed to see ya'll...so much pain has built up from Ashley's death. It's time to move on." Tears fell from his eyes. "How can I love anyone, when I'm harboring hatred in my heart." He shook his head in disgust. His father's hands against his neck stole his attention. Carl Edwards was standing there crying. "I'm sorry for what happened. I should've said that a long time ago, but a man's pride will keep him lost every time. Please forgive me." At that moment, the weight was lifted from Mikal's shoulders. All the money in the world could have done that. No worries, no problems, I was time to enjoy life. "Sit down old man and let's get caught up. "He laughed through his aches. *Cause everybody dies, but not everybody lives!*

CHAPTER FOURTEEN

CANDICE

"Mel where have you've been? You haven't returned any of my calls. Are you alright because you don't look like it?" Candice asked as she held the issue of Latina Magazine in front of her. Mel moved passed Candice with no words, in pre-Madonna mode which puzzled her. Since their recent visit from Ms. Johnson, Melvin had been acting strangely. In fact, nothing about him was the same. Candice raised from the table and followed him upstairs. Once there, she paused in the doorway, watching the man who looked nothing like the person he was. Blonde stubble basks his chin, dark rings outlined his eyes, telling the story of many nights with no rest. Melvin's clothes, which were usually fresh, were wrinkled and dirty. Sensing her presence, he turned to face her. His odor was overpowering the roses that left scents throughout the room.

"What you doing to yourself?" Candice asked. "I told you to slow down. There's too much ahead of us."

Melvin rolled his eyes and resumed filling his suitcases with his clothes. Silence charmed the room for about three minutes. Then he spoke to Candice. "Today is the end of my commitment to you. You're on your own from this day forward, but I'm going to need what you owe me and something to maintain my living standards." Melvin peeked from the closet to make sure she was listening. "I think $50,000 a month is enough."

"What?" Candice said. "Are you crazy? What did she tell you? That's too much money." Melvin stepped toward her wearing a devious grin. Dollar signs could be seen on both of his pupils. His constant sniffing displayed the effects the drugs was having on him. "She was right. You only care about yourself...nobody else is appreciated." Melvin ranted. "I did everything to get you here...even kept your secrets, but you don't appreciate it!"

"Mel don't listen to her. I appreciate you." Candice whispered.

"Candi, please...shut the fuck up...just accept who you are...which is a selfish bitch! Melvin pointed his finger toward her. He shook his head in frustration. "You'll pay me to keep my mouth closed about you and everything you've done." His fingers made a locking sign his lips. Candice pressed her hands against her chest, in shock. Her head was suddenly warm. *How could he do this!* She looked around franticly. *What should I do?"* This couldn't be allowed to happen. Melvin was in the closet, when Candice fully entered the room. In her hand was a crystal ashtray. He emerged and was met with the force of an object. His neck snapped back, sending his body in tow. Again, again and again, she swung connecting with his face, making blood splash over her arms and face.

None of that meant anything. Candice focused on the licks she was delivering to the man's head. No one would be allowed to ruin her pursuit to happiness. Tears dripped from her eyes as she stood huffing and puffing, over her victim. She studied the area. Blood was everywhere. Her shoulders sagged standing next to his dead body. He was dead without a shadow of a doubt. Candice released her clench to the ashtray. It was time to pull herself together. Candice ripped the sheets from the bed and covered him in them. She left but returned minutes later with Hefty trash bags. Pressing the small frame inside, she let herself relax. The next move was the shower. Her mind was spinning. Even though the blood was washing into the drain; the pain was still there. *Who was there to trust!*

Mikal popped to mind. How would he react? She knew the answer and that's why she wouldn't let it get back to him. All the sows scheduled, his reputation, everything was on the line. Something must be done. Candice exited the room. Strangely she felt no remorse. Then again why should she. After getting dressed, she returned and grabbed the bag. Stair after stair, Candice pulled the body to the lower level. No one was there when she peeked through the blinds of her rear entrance. Quickly, Candice pulled the bag to the awaiting car. She had to get as far away from this area as possible. Hopefully, nobody recognized her at one of these local motels. In the morning she would call Mikal and let him know she was alright. She sat down in the sofa. *Who could she trust?"*

There was one person she knew she could count on. The problem was, he was miles away, but what choice did she have. Her mind was running on automatic. A dead man was outside her home and all the evidence linking her to it was upstairs. If she wanted to survive this ordeal help was needed. Candice closed her eyes and massaged her temples. "Fuck it!" She said. The long-distance call too no time at all. "Yea," the man answered.

Candice began crying. "Jeffery, I need your help please." She continued to cry. "Can't get in touch with Salinas. Whatever you want I'll pay...just get here." Candice listened, then she relayed the information he asked for.

...The bottle smashed against Rosie's head, sending her tumbling to the floor. "Bitch chu' the reason he dat' way. Chu did it to him." Jualian yelled with all the strength of his lungs. She balled in a knot preparing for the next assault, but nothing came. Through the cracks in her arms, Rosie watched him leave the room. His footsteps echoed in the wooded hallway until it was replaced by the sound of a door closing. He was gone! Slowly, she raised to a sitting position causing the blood to leak from her wound into her face. Stiches would be needed. For some reason it hurt less with him gone. No tears formed and no painful aches. Crying was not the answer. *Strength!* Rosie stiffened when the bedroom door eased open and both pairs of eyes that were watching entered...

Banging on the motel door woke her from her sleeping slump. She rose and staggered to the door. Beds hitting against her legs jarred her all the way awoke. *Had he made it this quick?* Candice opened the door and Jeffery Hicks entered, wearing army gear and toting and big duffel bag. He dropped it in the middle of the floor. "I got on the highway as soon as I got off the phone with you. From the sound of things, something is seriously wrong."

Candice flopped down and placed her hands in her lap. This whole situation was spiraling out of control, but that was beside the point, it had to be taken care of soon Jeffery continued. "Yo' brother is doin' alright. Him and my daughter got a good thing goin' and it don't need none of yo' mess. He looked at her and shook his head. "It's yo' life, but don't be surprised if it come back on you. How long do you think you can keep foolin' people?"

Candice avoided the question. "Will you help me? I've been getting calls from my label, but I don't want to meet with them until I know for sure this is over and done with."

To him that sounded reasonable. "So, what's the problem?"

She pointed to the bag in the corner just behind him. His experience in the game told him what it was at first glance. Jeffery scratched his head. "I don't wanna ask, but what the hell have you done?" Candice opened up about everything. "Money's not the problem...I just...need it to disappear."

"Yo' momma is probably turnin' in her grave, knowin' how far your takin this deception. Give me the address to yo' condo. It's gonna cost you $100,000. Not a penny less. Send it to my daughters account. There's a few people I wanna check on while I'm here anyway." Jeffery thought abought his nephew, Doug.

"I guess it can't get no worse." But was he ever so wrong.

CHAPTER FIFTEEN

MIKAL

One of Dallas's most popular club owners, Ricky Smith, sat at the table of Hooters grappling with the idea of starting his own record label. He tosses the thought around to his surrounding team, which consist of Jarvis Ramsey and Preston Williams. They were the muscle behind his movements. When visits had to be made, they came. When bodies had to be drug, they did it. "J-Ram what you think about this?" Ricky asked. "I'm tryna' figure it out."

J-Ram displayed a single gold in his mouth. His frame resembled someone who frequently took trips to the gym. Dallas Cowboy's jumpsuit and an albino python covered his body. "Shidd," He started rubbing his facial hairs. "You been makin' smart moves so don't make a fucked up one now. Leave the silliness out the door." Big P agreed. "Yea don't do nothin' that ain't gonna make no funds."

Ricky bit down on his bottom lip. Witnessing the success of Street Approved Records, opened his eyes to the type of money performing could bring. The thought of competing against them had him hesitant because it could be suicide. "I know some niggas that be flowin' though." J-Ram said. He turned his attention to the reptile circling around his forearm. Ricky looked of in the distance, drumming his fingers against the side of the glass. His impatience was setting in. Mikal Edwards phone call was overpowering the way his day went. Ever since then, he only thought about the proper way to showcase those artists at his club. Tan Polo sport covered his medium size frame, as he leaned back.

Black diamonds hung from his ears, neck, and wrist area. This told the world that money was second nature. A flashback appeared in Slick Rick's head, repaying the escape from the life of the old. For the last year, him and his wife Tamika, was relaxing. Highway after highway, state by state, drained, but nevertheless the deal with the devil was complete. Surprisingly, their love had not dwindled. Mikal walked through the door with his shoulders slumped and face long. Ricky exhaled, as the man plumped down in the open seat at the table. It was going to be one of those days. His demeaner said that something was seriously wrong. "Man, what's up, and don't come in here with no bullshit. At least let it be cow shit because I've drove too far fo' that." Ricky looked toward his team and then smooth out his tapered haircut.

Mikal looked toward him with a slight grin. "What you got 99 problems and a bitch ain't one." He waved him off and searched for the waitress. "Sadly...that's the deal. My star player been missin' fo' three days."

"Three days!" Ricky raised up. "What kind of shit is that?" They'd been cool ever since they'd met at the car lot, when Mikal was purchasing his Lambo, about a year ago. From that day forward, Ricky was the go-to man for any local concerts. Mikal paused, then stood up and opened his arms. "Let's start over. Give me a hug and you're lookin' good too." They embraced. "How's wifey?"

Ricky smiled showing the in-crushed lower set of teeth. "We good...finally, through fuckin' with that hoe ass Mexican. She happy as hell cause she pregnant. Think that's gonna' slow me down." He gave a silly expression. "I'm glad you called me because the spot need some more concerts. It's been a minute."

"We had an agreement. It's just most of the time the artist is wanted out of town, so we would go to the money." Mikal said.

"She need's the Triple D supportin' her and that's gonna help our movement." He looked around the restaurant. It was crazy nobody was bothering them. That was a blessing. "Like I was sayin' though, my new artist Candi, she be on those billboards round town...well she ain't called back...her agent ain't called neither. I can't tell my CEO that shit, she'll go dumb. "Mikal rubbed his eyes.

"Yo' club is our first show. Bitch ain't answering texts or nothing" he smashed his fist against the table causing J-Ram's snake to jump.

"Damn, look at that hoe!" Ricky leaned forward waving at the woman. Within seconds Mikal located her. The sight startled him so bad, he jumped from his seat. "Candi!" "Yes, she is." Ricky adjusted his chain and looked at his boys, who was equally impressed. Her picture did no justice to the real sight.

"Nigga put yo' tongue back in yo' mouth, you married." Mikal teased.

Laughter erupted from their mouths! "What she doesn't know, won't hurt." Candice strutted toward them like a diva...the female definition of a hustler. Her honey stripped hair was wrapped tightly in a bun and only allowed two pieces of hair to hang loose, over her left eye. A Marc Jacobs single twist dress, with slits by both legs, looked as though it was painted on her body personally.

The woman's waistline brought emphasis to the deep arch that attached her nice size butt. Watching her walk was amazing. She stopped, hugged Mikal, and took the seat Big P gave her. "Sorry I didn't return your calls, very unprofessional on my part, but my brother and I had some problems that required my immediate attention in Chicago. I stayed in the Chicago South Loop Hotel if you'd like to check. I'll explain more later." Candice glanced toward Ricky and his crew. "My agent probably didn't tell you because I fired him." Candice lied. "I called Kim and here I am."

Mikal didn't speak for a while. "This Ricky. We were discussin' yo' first show." Ricky started laughing again, drawing stares from them both. He held up his hands when Mikal narrowed his eyes at him. "As I was sayin', too much goin' on. I want you to stay with me until we can get you situated. No strings attached just need this to work." Mikal continued, "There's too much fo' that bullshit."

Knowingly, she nodded. "Can we talk about this alone?" Candice sexy smile formed. "That's my key. Let's bounce fellows." Ricky stood and stretched his hands. "Be sure to call so we can get this mapped out." He touched Candice next. "Wish I could stay longer, but it was nice to meet you." "Damn sure is." J-Ram said with a wink that caused Big P to chuckle. Then like yesterday, they were gone. Both sat there until the timing felt right to speak. Mikal rubbed his hands together calmly. "Candi do you really want what's in front of you?"

"What kind of question is that?" Candice looked away trying to avoid those emerald green eyes. Even while angry, they were demanding attention.

"A question with a question. That's some new way of conversation."

"Alright Mikal," Candice replied. "Yes, I do...and this won't happen again. Please let's move on. I'm ready to do whatever." Mikal let the words rest in the air as he thought about the next move. He needed to feel what was taking place.

Never, has he taken a chance like this before, but Mikal refused to drag the label down. Too much was on his shoulders and the stars was his goal. A goal that many was scared to reach for, because the fear of failure. Instead, they picked a flower off the ground because it was in arms reach. That wasn't him.

"Do you feel comfortable stayin' with me fo' a time? My house is big, and it won't be a problem."

"No, I don't mind. As a matter of fact, I'd love too." Candice said seductively.

Mikal shook his head. "Business Candi."

"Of course, it's business."

Mikal started laughing. "Girl...let's get out of here. I'll show you where I stay, and you can go make arrangements to get things done. There's a lot of good things ahead of us."

Candice raised and grabbed his hand. "I already know."

CHAPTER SIXTEEN

CANDICE

Mikal's house was gorgeous in so many ways. For several days, Candice walked around admiring what he'd built. His decorating skills was better than most women she knew. The gigantic swimming pool by his guesthouse put emphasis on the whole lay-out. From the front yard to the back, peacocks and their mates, ran freely. Mikal's style was implemented on everything she saw.

KNOCK! KNOCK! KNOCK!

Candice moved quickly from the far side of the estate; when she heard the banging. The sound echoed through the hallway as they kept beating on the thick wooden door. Whoever it was refused to use the doorbell and that made no sense at all.

KNOCK! KNOCK! KNOCK!

She paused to look at the big tropical aquarium briefly. *Beautiful!*

Even though she'd lived here for a week, it was still eye-catching every time she saw it. Candice pressed her lips together in awe because this was a dream come true. The transaction with him was easier then she'd expected, but just the sight of him made things better. Candice swung the door wide. "Rachael!"

She said in shock.

"Yes, sweetie it's me." The woman pushed pass her. "Girl you need to hurry and get dress. Mikal sent us over here to take you shopping before we hit the road. This a good time for us to get to know each other." She sat down on the leather couch and crossed her legs. "Because he's paying."

"Well, let me hurry." Candice turned and raced toward the back room with Rachel yelling behind her. "Those chicks really don't like you. Hell, I don't either." She laughed. "How the heck you get to stay with him? He doesn't do that."

Candice entered the room wearing a pink Nike jumpsuit and matching shoes. "let's get going girl. I don't even know you and you in my business."

Rachel shook her head. "Really."

"Really." Candice countered.

They stepped out the house to where the Cadillac Escalade sat. "You might last after all." Two bodyguards opened the door and allowed them in. Moni's slant of the eye was the first thing that caught her attention.

01' my gosh! She wasn't a success and trouble, was stirring. Candice spoke. "Hello ladies, what's happening today?" Pam glanced, then continued fiddling with her nails. That baffled her how one man could drive a wedge through women that knew nothing about each other. Rachael was the only relaxed individual in the SUV. "Are you having fun?" Candice asked.

"Sure is." Was her response.

"Listen ladies." Candice began. "I'm Candi and we're on the same team. Don't make this a me or your situation because..." She studied each person. "...you will lose. So, let's make this work.'

The power of dick! Candice thought. "Turn that up please." Drake was singing the gospel. "I've been down so long; it looks like up to me/they look up to me, I got fake people showin' fake love to me/straight up to my face..." The song had so much merit. In the end hopefully, things would be right with themselves, but

117

that may be longer. As for now, it was time they knew she was ratchet too.

Their shopping spree turned into an autograph session as soon as they entered Valley View Mall. Candice was surprised at how man followers they had. Secret Confessions was in a class of their own. She stepped closer to Pam and spoke quietly. "Is this how it is all the time?"

Pam's smile moved up and down with her head. "Enjoy it while you can because you never know when it will end." That statement is true; something that punched against her skull daily. Candice looked around with glossy eyes. *Please be done with it!* She prayed inwardly. Both bodyguards made sure no one came to close. Both bodyguards made sure no one came too close. A tall handsome man bent down towards Candice. She stepped forward thinking he was another male groupie, but immediately that thought changed.

His posture said nothing of that. Wide legged, long hair, and Versace down, he stood there in full command. "I won't take up too much of yo' time because the longer I stand here; the more money walks away." His smooth smile appeared. He rubbed his chin and fluffed out his linen. "...unless you walkin' with me." The statement caught all the women attention.

They laughed in good spirit, making him kick forward his white gators. When it came to game, he was the blame because it was in his DNA. "What's up pimp?" Moni said gathering snickers from the crowd.

"I'm glad you recognize pimpin' when it's in yo' face." He wiped his finger across his lips. "...and you better stay cool cocoa befo' you get drunk up." Mr. Greedy smacked his lips.

Pam clapped her hands together. "What the hell- "the comment never finished.

"Baby I don't think yo' management doin' a good job because you need to be seen and not heard. That'll be money well spent."

"What's that mean?" She placed her palms on her hips.

"It means, I can't hear your mama, yo' status to short." The bodyguards urged him away, but that only encourage Mr. Greedy. "I'm real greedy and real great. If you don't participant, don't hate because this could be yo' big break." Mr. Greedy let himself smile when he saw the women bent over in laughter.

Rachael asked, "What do you want?"

Candice hugged him. "You earned this." She winked.

"All I want is to take a picture with you hoes on my shoulder." He revealed his diamond covered grill again.

"That way y'all can tell the world you met a celebrity."

That brought more cheers. The four women grouped around him. He was the turn of their day. It was fun to be around someone that was authentic. Once the pictures were taken, Mr. Greedy hugged them and strolled away. Pam looked over him while he walked. "Do you think pimpin' still alive?" Moni replied "If it is, we've just met one of Dallas's finest. Now can we finish shopping before somebody get copped." That brought smiles and giggles.

Candice entered the house hours later. Mikal was nowhere to be found. This had become his routine. He spent more time in the studio then his own home. The man lived and slept entertainment. Hard work and dedication were his motto. She headed to the back for a shower and a nap.

"Dr. Peters entered the room and sit down on the sofa. He studied his patient for a while. "This is a process every patient goes through. It's done to get a basic understanding of how your mind works. We have to know your mental state." A nod came from the patient. He continued. "Alright are you sure this is what you want to do? Once completed, there will be unfixing. We must know for sure this is it. If some more time is needed, please take it...I advise that." The psychiatrist doodled on his notepad.

"This is what I want. It's the only thing that makes me whole. It's what I've always wanted."

"But you're so young." Dr. Peters pitched n.

"I know. That's where it always starts, right?" The patient said. "I want to live out my dream as well as my mothers."

The slim man adjusted his glasses. "I can understand that. One more, is it scheduled before we actually..." Candice woke up in a cold sweat. Something had to be done about these dreams. They were bringing to many unwanted memories.

CHAPTER SEVENTEEN

MIKAL

Soft jazz played in the background of the newly modeled Italian restaurant, giving it the vibe of the old mafia days. Six weeks, morning, noon and night, twerking and re-twerking, music had drained him something terrible. Mikal worked for nothing less than perfection, but now sitting in front of Kimberly Jones, those traits weren't needed. Her brief glances, the way she spoke, and her high school personality, made him boyish, in a good way. To be able to relax in an environment filled with stuck up millionaires was not often accomplished. He watched the way she smooths the loose string of hair from her beautiful face. The sight took his mind elsewhere, mostly, dreaming of being pressed against the softness of her skin, enjoying her fragranced drifting through the air.

"You're so gorgeous Kim, but fo' some reason, I think you know that." Mikal observed the clothes she wore. The simplest muumuu looked unique on her body. Lake Como, which was the name of the eatery they were at, seemed like a setting for couples only. Deep inside, he knew the gift she possessed would change his life for the better. Mikal coached himself to be courageous tonight because winning her approval would take something bold. This was the moment. He unfastened his Versace jacket, revealing a fitted Oxford dress shirt. His eyes locked on hers and watched the signals fly between them. As hard as she thought, his emerald green pupils were hypnotizing. Kim watched without words. She could sense something major was brewing. Mikal stood abruptly. "Excuse me...please! Sorry to interrupt, but I'd like to ask somethin'."

What is he doing! Kim muzzled over the thought. He continued. "I know many of you came out tonight to be with yo' loved ones, to have intimate conversation, or to just get away." The statement brought smiles from the onlookers, so he paused for effect. "...How long do you wait until you reach fo' the person you want?"

Kim pursed her lips to keep from smiling. She noticed the crowd anticipating his next words. Romance was always welcomed by women and with this planned attempt, his future looked promising.

That toughness was put to a halt when Mikal removed his coat and sat it on the end of the chair. Two buttons strain to hold his well sculpted frame inside. Grabbing a flute of champagne, he sipped until the live band begin to play, then he sang, "baby I wanna' fly through a storm on a unicorn/make love on a mountain, want nothin' but our bodies keepin' us warm/I wanna' bathe in a fountain of wine/kiss 'til the mornin' time and watch you dance from behind..."

Cheers and applause grew louder. Kim's heart beats to the rhythm of his voice. It reminded her of the first time she was asked out to a Valentine party. Mikal pushed forward. "...Versace on the floor, makin' love on the front porch/feelin' yo' lips pressed against mine/this is just the beginning, but it won't be the last time." Kim clapped along with the audience as he sat back down. The short concert that was performed, held the feelings of the whole world...love!

"You're making this hard on me." Kim stated.

"That's my intention so why did you ask me here tonight?"

"Suddenly it doesn't matter." Kim replied with apparent lust controlling her body. Mikal laughed. "Business first, remember?" His perfect smile flashed. *How could she not want him?* He was the man every woman dream's of. Tall, dark, and handsome, and equipped with a career. "That was before this stunt." She fanned herself and studied the stares comin' their way. "I want what you want, but I want it to work. I haven't been with a man in three years."

Kim saw the shock in his expression and nodded. There was no need to relive the past. "It's been all about my son and the empire we've built. If we're going to step into this, let's make sure that it's correct." Boyz II Men changed the tune of the night as it came roaring through the speakers, placing them in a time of peace. No one was in a hurry to talk. Why should they? Both knew what was happening. Both knew the effect it could cause, but neither cared. They wanted the same thing, from the right person. Kim touched his face and kissed his lips. "Are you serious about flying through a storm on the back of a unicorn?"

"You like that?" He asked.

She inhaled. "Mikal take this slow. As bad as I want you, I want it to be more than one time. It's better for us that way." Kim leaned and closed her eyes, salvaging the feelings, but when she reopened them, it was back to business. "How far a long are you with this record?"

"I'm puttin' the finishin' touches on the last tracks now. Candi's ready. I got her in the studio day in and day out. You know how I am." Mikal grabbed his drink and sipped. "The other girls are just waitin' in the cut. When we're done, it's on."

Kim looked off. "There's something about that woman that doesn't sit right with me. What all do you know about her?"

"Everything on the surface, but why?"

She shrugged. "I'm not sure. Viper always said everyone a suspect until you're sure about what's around you. It's been my motto since his death, but I'm a woman and it just feels wrong...everything." Kim shook her head.

"Well let's enjoy the rest of the night, there's too much to smile about." Mikal winked.

"Yes, there is." Kim kissed him again. "I never knew how much I missed this."

"I told you nigga!" Mikal yelled through the phone. "I'm always gonna' get what I want." He chuckled. Two guys caught his attention while he was talking. It was 2 o'clock in the morning and he was on the other side of town, out of place.

After Kim and him parted, Mikal chose to drive around Dallas and enjoy the win for a while. She had so much that other women didn't have. Her characteristics was so close to his sisters, it was scary. "What nigga?" Me and Kim decided to give us a chance, but I must be careful because she ain't like the rest of these hoes. I can't lie, I hit the lottery baby." He listened to A.J. on the other end. It's official yo' boy is back." Laughter. His excitement didn't answer why he was sitting in the parking lot of Turtle Creek Drive, with no weapon. Mikal search through his mirrors for the men, who'd disappeared in the dark trees.

A Bentley coupe represented money and the streets kept people needing some.

NAP! NAP! NAP!

The glass of his car sounded, making him turn to meet the barrel of a .45 automatic. *Damn It!* Mikal slowly rolled down the window. "I don't need any trouble lil brother." His palms returned to the safety of the wood grain wheel, but the hunger in their eyes, told him it wouldn't be that easy.

"It doesn't work like that. I'm gonna give the orders and you gonna follow them. Gone get out balla." The men surveyed the road nervously. Their faces were visual, but that made no difference, if he was dead when the police arrived. "Listen fellow, I've had a lot to drink, the nights been long, let me give you the ten racks in my glove compartment and we move on... no harm done. I'll take this as a learnin' experience." The second man smiled but didn't agree. "I know you. You from Street Approved Records. Naw dawg, we need you out the ride. It's better that way."

Mikal opened the door and slid out. He stood four inches taller than both, but the gun was the equalizer. "Man, ten racks a good come up." Mikal suggested. "I wish I had more, unless the watch will help? I'm just trying to walk away in one piece." That made one of the men laugh. *One step closer!* Mikal kept talking. "Y'all won't get far in the Bentley because it has a built in GPS."

"But we can- "In one swift motion, Mikal snatched the gun and delivered a powerful roundhouse kick to the odd man's head. That gave some time to position himself for the fight that was to come. They rushed him at the same time causing him to stumble back and forward. His body bumped against the car, stopping his retreating room. He locked his arms like Jon Jones and sent a rib crushing combination. Mikal's first punch went to the attacker's solar flex, then followed by a blow to his short rib and capped off with a reverse elbow to the head. *Down goes Frazier!* He thought.

The assault happened so quickly the second man didn't have a chance to react. He stood there paralyzed. "I'm gonna give you the opportunity to get yo' partna' and get out of dodge or we can see where this will end?" He tilted his head toward the cement. Footsteps faded in the distance before another word was said. As funny as the sight was, Mikal didn't laugh. A life threating situation like this had no humor involved. He fumbled in the backseat until the gun was in his hand. With one swift throw, it landed in the water of Turtle Creek. He got back in the car and bagged out. The man's silhouette in the shadows made him pause. Sadness filled his heart at that moment. What a person wouldn't do to get ahead in this dirty world was crazy. Mikal tossed the money on the ground next to the man. Hopefully the blessing would help him appreciate life more because one day it might not end so well.

Early the next morning, Mikal woke to the sound of Candi's soft mumbles. He thought about her for a while. Her condo was still unprepared and the urge to have sex with her was taking its toll. *Power of pussy!* He raised and headed to the shower, but the noise made him detour. Mikal peeked out the door and the mumbles grew louder. It was strange because of the location. He walks down the hall with nothing, but his boxer briefs on. He listens to Candi once in the room. Her words were scattered apart so he moved closer. Kim had him suspicious for no reason. The sight of Candi's breast jumped out at him. Her light brown nipples sat erect as she lay on her back, across the couch. His eyes traced her body, forgetting what was happening. See through panties was controlling his, now hard penis.

Mikal shook his head. He never knew how sexy she was in the nude. With a body so intoxicating, the distant cries were fading away. He watched her fist tighten and open, making her look like she evil in a way. Mikal looked in horror. What was wrong with her? He stepped closer and kneeled. "Candi," His words were soft. "Candi," He said again. Her oval shaped eyes open and before he responded, she embraced him, pressing her warm body and soft breast against his chest. "You're havin' a bad dream. It's alright." Mikal assured her. He could feel the wetness from her tears. "Everything goin' to be alright just relax."

"I'm sorry." Candice cried. "I'm so sorry."

Mikal gave no reply. "Sorry fo' what!"

CHAPTER EIGHTEEN

CANDICE

Life isn't always fair! That statement was the only thing in her mind, while the phone pressed against her ear. Nothing is ever over just readjusted, when it comes to living. Over, refers to the casket closing and the people that love you saying their last prayers. That's when it's over and Candice wasn't ready for that. There was too much left to experience. "Our plans have been detoured...my job fo' you, will call fo' a job from you." It was an order. Candice stared at her mirror reflection in his secluded bathroom at the back of Mikal's house. Horror had replaced her reality she wanted desperately to conceal it from him. That thought made her want to crawl into bed with him, so she could feel safe again. He was her security. Jeff continued, breaking those thoughts. "I think it would be better if we met to talk again."

Candice thought about running or hiding underneath a rock, but what would that change. As soon as she emerged, the same problems, the same people and the same scenario would be presented. *What could be wrong!* All his money was timely deposited so why wouldn't he leave her be. "Explain why we need to talk?" She tried to be strong but trying was easier than being.

Jeff sighed through the receiver, then went into a drawn-out story, with no reference to the situation. "My mother worked two jobs and my father was a military man that done what needed to be done to fend fo' his family. One day he just walked away. I learned a lot as a child about life at that time, was never answered. He left a wife and three kids. Why did that happen? Everything happens fo' a reason...why did you call me?

"The picture I took of yo' place in only fo' collateral. Right now, we're the only two that know anything. Let's keep it that way and you can have yo' little happy life." The threat served its purpose. Hatred stemmed in Candice mind as she listens. Jeff pushed forward. In order fo' this to vanish, one thing is required..."

Puzzlement stumped itself across her head. "What do you want from me and how do I know you won't return after this?"

"You don't, but it's less likely."

Candice paced back and forth in the bathroom. "What do you want?" Her heart beat was the only noise to be heard. Everything around her was as quite as a midnight grave yard.

"Kimberly Jones, the owner of yo' record label..." Jeff replied. "I want to know where she's keepin' her son."

Candice was confused. "Why?"

"There's a lot you don't know about that label and your position put me in the mix that I need to get some..." He went silent. "Maybe one day I can tell you, but as of now, do what I asked." Her eardrum felt the pounding of the dial tone which told her that he had hung up.

"What have I done?" The words streamed out. During her course of planning, this was never a part of the plan. No incident could compare to this stage. *Melvin!*

Through the hard times he was her trust. Her family didn't accept her, only her mother, who was dead. Candice shook her head in frustration. Melvin's drug habit destroyed what they built. He was nowhere near the smart intelligent person she knew at the time. They both knew what was ahead, but poisoning his mind, interrupted what was to come. Melvin knew too much. *He had to go!* She reasoned.

In his death, the man was still annihilating her career. Temperatures was rising indescribable. Something had to be done to stop this. Street Approved Records made it clear that nothing would come in the way of the progression of the company. If a breeze of her drama crossed TMZ's desk, she could kiss her life goodbye. Getting information about Kim's son would be harder than penetrating the White House. The woman wanted her child to have nothing to do with this life at this moment. Jay Z and Beyoncé was the only people that could compare to the security she had on her son. *What was so important about this!* Candice was stupid, something big was happening and she needed to find out what it was. Mikal's handsome features took control of her thoughts. She had to get that out her mind to think straight.

She excited the bathroom and walked toward his room. Reaching his area, Candice, lightly knocked on his door. She waited a few minutes, then tapped again, causing the door to crack faintly. Candice peeked inside at the plushed room. Cherry Oak wood furniture captivated her eyes. Mikal laid on his back in a king size bed, exposing a six-pack stomach. With the sheet hanging low, she could imagine what the rest of his body looked like. The buck of his chest combined with large shoulders and thick arms was mesmerizing. Candice bit down on her fingernail. Through all the drama in her life, he symbolized peace and tranquility. She stepped deeper in the room. *Be bold!* Her tiny tank top and black boy shorts was the only clothing she wore. Candice moved closer and paused at the edge of his bed. She examined his dark flesh like a hawk ready to attack.

A man of his caliber was hard to concur but now she had the chance. She inhaled his scent and enjoyed every second of it. Unconsciously, Candice begin to rub her breast, making her nipples stand erect. She wanted him more than ever before. Hair lined his stomach disappearing beneath his boxers. *Be bold!* She told herself. She kneeled next to the bed and reached under the sheet, where his limp dick rest. Even soft, it was bigger than her palm. She watched his reaction as she caressed his manhood. It begins to grow. Candice gently removed the covers to get a better look. She was surprised to find that he was uncircumcised. That fact made him more attractive. He was still natural, regardless of the money he possessed, but that thought faded when the vein started traveling down his ten inches. Her body begin to tingle and his did the same as she motioned up and down his dick with her small hand. His body tensed.

Candice knew the moment had taken control of him. Filling her mouth with saliva she wrapped her lips around his dick and begin massaging his shaft with her lips. Up and down, slow and gentle, up and down was the tempo she used. Mikal's eyes opened and watched Candice. She sucked his dick, stopping at the tip the way he liked it. Confusion was in his eyes, but the feeling of her sloppy blow job had him unable to react. He wanted to tell her to stop. Kim was who he wants, but her pretty lips stole the words from his mouth. Candice moved up and down pausing to give him eye contact. She rubbed his balls making moans escape his throat. He watched as his large dick lay on the side of her face. It was almost the length of her head. "Candi...please stop. We're not 'spose to do this." His words faded away as she swallowed half of his dick.

She begins to move faster and faster. She wanted to taste his cum in her mouth. A sudden push sent her backwards to the floor. Shock was painted on her beautiful face. "We can't do this. You need to leave, and I'll have you a place to stay by this afternoon." Mikal raised up and headed to the bathroom, leaving her with her thoughts. Minutes passed before she could gather herself from the floor. The embarrassment on her face turned into a smile once she retrieved her cellphone. She pressed a button to see if the footage was there. Smiling broadly, Candice pushed stop and save. His anger toward her made the mission less painful. *I got it handsome!*

CHAPTER NINETEEN

MIKAL

Kim looked up from her computer when she heard the sudden sound of her office door, slamming. Everything on her desk raddled from the impact of the mahogany frame. Slowly, she spent her chair around to face Mikal, as he flopped his 230 pounds down in the open seat across from her. His facial expression showed frustration and that made Kim concerned because he was a person that masked his emotions well. Plus, this was the second time, in as many weeks, that he'd come came to speak with her about something that was bothering him. She couldn't rid the thought of the attempted robbery. Kim picked up her Fendi bag and removed her palm mirror. She was self-conscious of her appearance every time he came around.

She pulled her wavy hair back to reveal the unique structure of her neck lining. Her caramel skin tone enhanced the power of her beauty, which seemed to drive men wild. "What's wrong Mikal?" She asked as she removed her suede jacket to the blue powder Marc Jacobs pants suit. Kim watch as he looked over her breast but said nothing. The shirt emphasized the firmness of her 34D chest. She watched him closely; something was definitely wrong. Mikal looked away and spoke. "I think you might be on to somethin'."

Wrinkles invaded her pretty features. She had no clue at what he was talking about. Noticing her confusion, he added. "Candi tried to suck-give me some head." He couldn't bring himself to say she had his dick in her mouth. It would be impossible to explain.

"I want to talk about it but- "Mikal shook his head and briefly made eye contact, then immediately returned his glance to the floor, where his white Gucci loafers sat. "I moved her in a condo in Plano, Texas now, but the strange part about it is ever since you said that. I've been noticin' things. I walked up on her talkin' in her sleep...cryin' fo' no reason. That's crazy, all you beautiful women have issues." He smiled,

Leaned back and rubbed his head. Mikal wasn't sure about anything. Too much was happening and something in his gut was telling him it wasn't right. "I don't know, maybe I'm overreactin'." He wiped the sweat from his hands on his cream linen pants.

Kim came from around the desk when she saw his shoulders slump. She stood at the rear of him.

"Mikal relax," Kim touched his tense neck. Her small fingers worked against the tension in his muscles.

"We'll figure it out. Candi is the right look, attitude and all...she has what we need to make a power move in the industry." She teased his ear with her tongue and massaged deeper into his stiffness. Mikal's body loosened up and again she pecked his ear. "Use your better judgment. Everything you've touched has turned to gold I trust your decision. I trust you Mikal in a way I haven't trusted any man since Viper died. He used to coach me to follow my instincts. That's what I've done with the label and Jibril.

They my world."

Mikal cuffed her tiny hands on his shoulders. That was special to him because Kim kept her personal life separated from this side of the world. By mere mention of her son, told him their relationship was moving in the correct direction. "I just don't want to bring any bullshit to this label. We movin' right and I want to keep it that way. I also found another rapper that goes by the name Mafia. He spits like that boy Twista."

"That's good. Keep doing what you're doing."

"I need to talk to Moni. Have you seen her?"

Kim smacked her lips and regretted it immediately. "Yes, um, why you are looking for her?"

Mikal stood and turned toward her. His large frame engulfed Kim's small body. "Please tell me you're not jealous? This is another side of Kimberly Jones." The closer he moved, the louder his heartbeat became.

BUMP! THUMP! BUMP! THUMP!

The sound was controlling her thoughts making her body imitate the rhyme. She rested her palms on his white linen shirt where his abs pushed against her hands. Kim caressed them as he unbuttons it. *What am I doing!* When the shirt fell to the floor, she explored his body, stopping at the bulge in his pants. Her lust couldn't be hidden. "Mikal this- "He smothered her words with his mouth.

"I won't do anything you don't want." He scooped her from the floor effortlessly and placed her on top of the desk. Then he removed her pants, allowing the opposite side to hang loose on her leg. Mikal wasted no time attacking her body with his mouth. For years, he'd dreamed of tasting her juices and now Kim's shaved pussy stared at him. He admired it, trying to decide the best way to put his lips to work. "Mikal please." Her faint cries fell on deaf ears.

His tongue touched the moist slot between her legs forcing a soft moan to fill the room. He watched as she maneuvered her hips to present him better access to her vagina. Mikal continued to mentally stimulate her body. He licked every hole but focused most on the clitoris. He teased inside, Kim gasped, fighting back her scream. She had to remember they were still in her office. Mikal spread her ass cheeks and dipped his saliva around the rim of her anus. Kim grabbed his head and begin to grind. His motions were driving her wild. "Mikal...it's been ...so long...um, yes baby...um, don't um...I'm Cumming."

Mikal sucked harder. He wanted to taste the sweet poison seeping from her body. His tongue flicked quicker, as she bumped her pussy into his face. She was literally fucking his mouth.

"Mikal...01' gosh...Mikal I'm...their baby...Yeesss!" Kim watched him swallow what dripped free. She closed her eyes until her body stopped trembling when she reopened them, he was standing over her dressed. The smile he held made her feel bashful. "As bad as I want to fuck you. I can wait. This is only a sample." His green eyes made Kim look away. They were overpowering. She fixed her clothes and hopped off the desktop. Her smile met his. "We CANNOT bring this type of...stuff into my work place." She wiggled her finger at him, then kissed his lips. "Now I have to leave early because my panties are a mess." Kim playfully punched him in the chest.

"That makes two of us...pre-cum is drippin' down my leg. I must go because there's somethin' I need to check out. Will you call me later?"

She bit her lip. "You're trying to turn me out, but I can't wait. Yes, is the answer to your question?"

Mikal's laughter could be heard in the hallway after he closed the door. Kim looked at the cum puddle on her desk." What have I done? Giggles.

Mikal entered Crushed Berries in deep conversation. His phone was pressed against his ear when the dim lighting of the club, made him pause. "Why you so surprised that I called?"

"Because it's usually me calling you. That's why."

"Well, today is different. I, um, wanted to talk to you and I need your help. If that's not a problem?" Mikal tilted his head toward a couple of security personnel and continued his walk to the rear office. Once there, he tapped a few times and waited." Secondly, I wouldn't mine pressin' my body against yours again, you feel me?"

Giggles exited the receiver. "You sure know how to pump my blood. I was planning to come back to Dallas next weekend, but what can I help you with?"

Ricky opened the door to allow entrance. Mikal acknowledged him with another head gesture, then pointed toward his phone.

"We'll have to finish this conversation later because I'm walkin' in a meetin' as we speak...just keep me on yo' mind."

"Um, huh, how can I forget you and that big ass dick." Mikal shook his head. He couldn't believe the way she talked. It didn't fit her looks at all, but this was her from top to bottom. "Woman," Laughs. It was the only way to shake the thought from his head. "Keep that in mind just in case you don't call back." He disconnected the line. "Slicksta what's the damn deal baby? Have you thought about my deal? I made sure all the paperwork was faxed to you myself."

"Yea I received them." Ricky shuffled through the papers on his desk. "Here we go. You said the first concert is February 14th. Why so far away?"

"There's so much goin' on, I have to give myself some room to work." Mikal crossed his legs.

"That's the best I can do at the moment."

"You want somethin' to drink?" He walked to his personal bar and poured a glass of Moet. At the sight of Mikal refusal. Ricky made another glass anyway. "Here nigga all that square shit up in here." Mikal accepted. Ricky begin talking again. "Do we still get Candi?" That woman is America's Most Wanted right now. The single got everybody lookin' fo' her."

Mikal sipped his drink and took a deep breath. "Yea she's still apart of the concert, but I have to check somethin' out. She took off faster than I thought possible."

"That hoe bad nigga. What you expect?" Ricky said. "What's really on yo' mind? I've been in the streets to long to be fooled by yo' fake ass act."

Mikal had to laugh. As of late, he wasn't doing a good job hiding things from people. "I need yo' help on a deeper level. Do you still have some power in the streets?"

Ricky shrugged.

"Awright Candi said some stuff in her sleep that got me wonderin'. I must investigate it before I make a wrong decision. She mentioned Kim's son...at least that's what sounded like. Then somebody name Rosie."

"So, what are you askin' from me?"

"I'm not sure. Can you put some people on her? I haven't told Kim because she'll go crazy. I must make sure I have some facts before I do that. I want to make sure I'm not trippin', feel me baby?

"That's what's up. Chill I got the man fo' the job." Ricky picked up the phone and dialed. "Danny Boy come to the spot. I want you to meet somebody and hurry up because it's important."

CHAPTER TWENTY

CANDICE

Drums pounded in her head from the nervousness of her heart. Her legs moved swiftly down Commerce St. I downtown Dallas. Left to right, Candice looked to make sure no one noticed her as she hustled toward the last building on the road. The cold air was the perfect cover-up needed to hide herself in public from the many new groupies chasing after an autograph. She had to get in and out. This was the only way her life would move forward. Pausing, Candice checked her phone for the message sent to her the night before. BRING NOBODY! Was the only thing she kept noticing? How could she? Explaining everything was too complicated. Not many people would understand what she was up against. "No, one," Candice whispered in the wind.

A glass sliding door stared at her while she stood on the pavement of the address. There was no other option left, but to go inside. She toyed with her black hair wrapper, to distract herself from the people, passing by at an alarming pace. The weather carried no friends this morning...except her. Candice stuffed her hands deeper inside the pockets of her black trench coat. Her designer shades hide her eyes as she studied the windows of the nearby buildings. This helped her embrace the freeze because her heart understood the feeling. Since a child confusion had become reality and her biggest façade came from the fight within. It was difficult being different when answers weren't available. Standing there, horns from the passing cars gave her life meaning, why she didn't know.

Candice looked at her reflection waving against the glass and wondered why the beauty she held couldn't be seen. Her outer view was the only thing present. Nobody cared about the problems traveling through her head. All they cared about was the feeling she brought. She looked around one final time, then walked in the lobby. A Hispanic receptionist greeted her when she approached. "Hello, how's your day going? It seems to be getting colder by the minute."

"I was thinking the same thing. Texas weather is so moody; you'd think it was one of us." Candice gave the lady a friendly smirk. "I've lived in New York for some time and it's one way or the other." She removed her glasses.

The plain faced woman's eyes grew large once she recognized who was standing in front of her. Candice shook her head aggressively and placed a finger to her lips. "Please, I'm just visiting a friend and I don't need all the excitement of the media. If you promise to keep this quiet. I'll send you tickets to my next concert."

A slow now came from the woman's head. Shock was covering her face and overtaking her ability to think. Candice touched her hand in hopes of calming the situation. "Let me go. Remember..." Again, she placed a finger to her lips and mouthed the words THANK YOU. Jeffery Hicks was waiting at the door when she knocked.

Candice stopped inside the room and immediately felt the negative energy floating around. She calculated the problem, but this was nothing like the doctor she'd controlled from the start. Jeffery Hicks' mind didn't rotate off lust. He was a man that knew what he wanted and how it should be accomplished.

Candice took her coat off and moved toward the empty seat in front of him. *Let the game begin!* She thought. "Glad you could make it. I was startin' to think you wouldn't." Uncle Jeff glanced at the clock on the wall. "Have a look at these." He handed her a folder filled with pictures and newspaper clippings. Candice poured the contents in her lap and rambled through them. A young man lay dad on the floor of a courtroom. The headline read: SUICIDE INSTEAD OF PUNISHMENT. Confusion entered her brain as she continued looking through the pictures. Melvin's battered face, along with pictures of her condo, appeared. All the photographs reminded her of NCIS: LA. He started talking again as she studied the pictures. "The man in the olive-green suit is my nephew. He committed suicide years ago. The original owner of that label your signed to is the infamous Vince McDavis, Viper. My nephew was a part of his death.

"I asked fo' yo help because I have some unfinished business to tend to. A man can't move forward knowin' somethin' is still behind him." Candice replaced the material. "It's been sometime since this happened and the wound never closed Doug was like my own." Uncle Jeff looked off. "I have to do somethin'." The words came out low, leaving pain chasing behind them. Questions filled Candice's mind but how could she ask. Why was Kim's son whereabouts so important? That thought shortly relived. "A son fo' a son in the conclusion I came too." Uncle Jeff replied. That mere statement changed her perception of what she was up against. Now she was not only scared for herself but for the child. What child should pay for their parent's wrong? She could think of none. "Find this information or else."

Uncle Jeff walked to the door and opened it. Candice nodded her head as she buried her body back in the long coat she'd wore. Placing the folder underneath her arms, she stepped into the hallway and stopped.

Candice turned to face him.

The man was heartless as the one person she'd hated... her father. It matters none that her brother was his son in law. All he cared about was revenge. His wrinkled skin, distant eyes and dead soul left nothing to the imagination. This was a deal with the devil and there was no canceling it. They stared into each other's eyes; no one blinked. Candice left knowing the only way this would end, was with one of their heads sleeping by a tombstone. Somehow, he had to be eliminated.

Dirt stained the man's clothes from the ground he'd made his home. He stood up to the frowns of people passing him by. Homeless people were used to those stares, but not him. The fact that humans could be treated so unkind made him mad. He watched Candice stroll back up Commerce to where her car was located. She'd been inside the building for just over an hour. He removed his phone and took several pictures to show her whereabouts. *Who was she visiting!* That question needed an answer. Once he was sure Candice had driven away from the area, the self-made homeless man returned to the spot he calls home. His bucket, sign and army bag sat next to him as he waited. The man positioned his phone, so he could take pictures of whoever exited the building. They would find out what was going on.

CHAPTER TWENTY-ONE

MIKAL

Music flowed through the studio, as he concentrated on the 808's and drums in front of him. Mikal needed the singers to coexist with the sounds of his production. He listened to Pam carefully while she sung her notes. Mikal was taken by storm at the way she was placing passion in every word. The collaboration was bringing tears in his eyes. He wasn't sure if it was the song they were singing or the fact that his emotions was out of whack with life. Whichever case. Secret Confessions was painting the pictures of love like everyone wanted to see. "Boy, turn the lights down/and let's get closer then we normally do/my body is callin' your name/Please hurry and get on it, cause you're driving me insane. I know what you really want from me/I know, I know/...and the world don't understand." I know."

Mikal looked through the one-way window in awe. It was like a live show and he was the only person allowed to witness. They wanted to succeed and that's what he'd preached from day one. His words had finally set in.

Nothing could compare to them and that effort showed why they were the countries best-selling female group. "Ladies I couldn't ask fo' anything better than that. As bad as I want to, I can't thank ya'll." He saluted them and blew a kiss their way. The lightening in the room brighten with the press of button. "The passion, the energy, the everything...sounded so beautiful." Secret Confessions had his inter soul. This was the first time they'd rehearsed, and no mistakes occurred. His picky personality made things harder by the day, but this time they'd nailed it, giving nothing to complain about.

Let's take a break and meet back at, um," He glanced at his watch. "...one thirty." The women exited the booth at the same time the studio intercom erupted. He grabbed Moni's hand and held her in place because as of late, the woman's actions were becoming bolder. Several uninvited visits, late night calls and naked pictures sent to his phone was becoming unacceptable. The surfacing rumors of Kim and his relationship was not only in the papers but terrorizing the office building. That fact seemed to make Moni more ambitious with her approaches. "Mr. Edwards, there's a package at the front that requires your signature to be received." Ms. Allen from the lobby area said over the speakers. Mikal looked toward Moni, who was playful batting her eyes toward him. She thought this was a game that she could possibly win. He shook his head. "You haven't gotten away. What you're doin' must stop, fo' real ma."

"Why because Miss Fancy is in the mix now." She waved him off. "You love to fuck too much to pass up something as fine as me." Moni licked her tongue around her lips.

Mikal observed her slender, well portioned, frame and bit into his lip. The way her Chanel leopard suit hugged her body made his heart skip a beat. There was no denying that she was interested in every way a man could think of, but the pros and cons didn't add up. "It ain't that but poppin up unannounced ain't gonna keep happenin'. If you still wanna play this game, it has to be by my rules or no more...period." He watches as she digested the words in her head. Moni knew he was serious from the way he spoke. Her persistence had knocked Pam out the way her plan was to do the same to Kim. That would never happen though.

"Think about this and we'll talk about it some more once I return." He let those words linger in the air as he departed.

His trip to the front desk took less than five minutes and now he was sitting in his office with a large envelope in his hands. Mikal poured the contents out and looked through them. Candice could be seen in many of the shots, even with the disguise she was wearing. Who was all the other people coming out of the building? It didn't make sense to him now. Nobody looked familiar. Quickly Mikal search the envelop again and found a brief notation. After reading it, he leaned back and closed his eyes. All the blood seems to drain from his face and into his feet. People talked about the secrets this label hides, but no one said anything that was threatening. This was a case of Murder INC, all over again. Mikal made up his mind. Kim would have known what's going on and how she was involved. He pushed a button, giving him direct access to her quarters. "Yes, Mikal is there something wrong because you never use this line?"

His words stumbled free. "Um, I, um, need to talk to you immediately…in my office." Breathing was the only sound he heard over the phone before she agreed. When Kim stepped inside his office, she begins questioning him. "What's wrong Mikal?" I can hear it in your voice." She looked at the photographs laying on his desktop. Kim stepped closer to get a better angle. "These was sent to me. Do you know anyone on them?"

Her eyes grew wide when she nodded. "Where did you get these from?"

Mikal held nothing back. In order to get answers, information had to be relayed. They were in a complex situation. "Who are they"

"There's no they...it's a e. His name is Jeffery Hicks and he was a part of Viper's death. Well not him but his nephew, who killed himself in court. I have to contact Tracy." Kim searched the room franticly like someone was hiding in the walls.

Mikal stood and embraced her. "Everything is goin' to be alright. Calm down and let me help you like I've already started doin'." He kissed her forehead. "I need fo' you to tell me what happened and how he fit. I'll deal with the rest. There's no need to call Tracy right now. Where is your son?"

"Tracy has him in Miami, why? What does he have to do with anything?"

"I'll explain that later, but we need to talk."

Kim hugged him tighter. "Alright, but what does Candi have to do with this?"

"That's the biggest question of all."

CHAPTER TWENTY-TWO

CANDICE

"This can't be happening." Candice told herself. She was alone in her condo trying to make sense of her situation. Her phone chirped while it reloaded the 30 second film of her giving Mikal oral sex. The sight was provocative but showed little dealing with the real reaction that transpired. She knew that this data linked into the wrong hands could damage his reputation. Candice face appeared on her screen once the programming stopped. She watched the video and every time she saw it, the same thing happened to her body. Mikal was the type of person she needed to have in her life, but Candice knew he'd never accept her past. He was a man that she'd never encountered. She walked toward her full-length mirror and studied herself.

To get the results that she carried took more money than Candice cared to recall. Her body was perfect to the naked eye, but stripped bare, there was a lot of confusion inside. The money she received from her mother's death helped with the self-esteem problem she'd lived with long ago. Candice was a woman that any man would want. She shook her head. Her mind drifted back ten years prior. That was the last time she saw her mother and father in under the same roof. He entered the chapel with his clothes reeking of alcohol and cigarette smoke. They possessed stains that looked like they were weeks old, and his boots held chunks of mud around the rims. Frowns came from everywhere, but that did nothing to discourage him from approaching his wife's casket. Jualian closed his eyes and gave what could pass for a prayer.

Candice stood in the distance and watched, too afraid to say a word. She hated him more than she cared to admit. One reason, Candice couldn't stop fearing him. Her father opened his eyes and searched around the church until he found her. His piercing stare made her shiver inside. Never had she felt so out of place. The words that left her father's mouth hurt now than it did at that time. "I will never accept you and what you've done." Then Jualian Galvez spit in her face. Candice remembered him walk away as spit slid down her cheek to the floor. People watched in horror, too scared to intervene. Her family tried desperately to calm the situation but was having little success. He had done it again. It never failed with him when it came to destroy her life.

She looked on as he stumbled out the door, undisturbed, down the aisle and out the door, where he shot himself in the head two blocks away. *Was any of this worth it!* Candice questioned herself then, only to be left with the same question years later. She'd lost both of her parents on the same day and that had torn her family in two. Many of them choosing not to speak of their reasons. Everything surfaced, from the day, she kissed that little boy underneath the bleachers, at school at the age of 8. There had to be away to fix this problem without sacrificing her integrity again. Candice knew she couldn't be a part of Jeffery Hicks plan to hurt an innocent child.

She walked back to her sofa and sat down. Her life was spiraling out of control at a fast pace. There had to be a solution. If not for her, for Mikal and that child...even if it meant losing all she worked for. This was the time to make her life mean something. Mikal was a part of a growing empire like Luscious and Cookie, but Kim's connection to this man's target was placing him in harm's way. She couldn't let that happen. Candice grabbed the bottle of pills off her table and swallowed three quickly. This was the only way she'd been able to rest as of lately. In no time at all her eyes became heavy and her mind traveled back to the days she hated so dearly...

"Get up baby, Get up please." The woman's voice kept whispering in his ear. When he began to move slow, she scooped him up and rubbed his curly hair. He needed protection from the monster. Rosie pressed his head down, so she could grab the bags from the floor. They had to leave this place for their safety.

"Where's Bubba?" The child asked, using his brother's nickname.

"He's waiting on us. We have to go." Carlos became strong. His little brother needed him.

KNOCK! KNOCK! KNOCK!

Candice jumped to her feet and looked toward the clock on the wall. Three hours pasted since sleep had taken control of her.

KNOCK! KNOCK! KNOCK!

Whoever was pounding on the door was becoming more aggressive. She slowly walked to the sound. Her mind was off balance from the effect of the drugs. It took all her strength to think straight. She disliked feelings this way, but it was the only way she could get those thoughts out of her head.

KNOCK! KNOCK! KNOCK!

"Alright already! I'm coming...gees." Candice yelled at the door. She twisted the knob and opened it without hesitation. Two masked men rushed inside the room, pushing her to the floor hard enough to knock her breath out. She tried to look up but was met with a punch in the eye. One set of hands placed her in restrains, while the other set smothered her with a wet cloth. Candice fought to stay conscious, only to find darkness approaching with every breath. *Help me!* Floated through her head before she went into another deep sleep.

A leather gloved hand slapped her face several times. The man continued to hit her until she started to respond. "I told you, you used to much of that shit nigga." One said.

"Shidd I don't know how much to use, but at least she alive." The second laughed. Candice thought she was dreaming when she heard the voices followed by Snoop Dogg rapping, Gin & Juice in the background, over the speakers. That soon told her she was still in bondage 's and held captive. She looked around at the brick walls that had equipment hanging from the hook. "Where am I?" She asked herself. On the floor were boxes of old packages that had Goodwill wrote across them. The sight told everything she needed to know to understand where she was.

Street Approved Records! Candice said to herself. Her eyes looked over her clothing and noticed that she still wore the same boy shorts and shirt that she had on at her condo. Her mouth was still stuffed so there was very little she could say to anyone. Candice took that time to watch. She heard Mikal's voice. That meant he was somewhere near. If she could only talk to him, it would help with what was going on. Kim stepped in front of her and the look on her face said the fairy tale she was living was over. *What did she know?* "I'm not here for games, so if you have any, I suggest you keep them concealed. How do you know Jeffery Hicks?" Her 5'2 statue seemed to grow twice the size. "I want to know what my child has to do with anything or you'll never leave this place alive...Candice, Candi or would it be better if you explain who Carlos is."

CHAPTER TWENTY-THREE

MIKAL

Life has many obstacles and to understand them, you must experience the short coming that's connected. At times, they seem surreal, but as the tables turn, situations take more of a movie effect. Mikal held the basement door open for his female friend. For years, their relationship was pure sexual and yet he still calls her in his time of need. He watched while she strolled by him. Long yellow legs, small waist, and nice ass. Those things made way for the beauty that attracted him with every step. Her Gucci Bamboo perfume lingered in the air, taking his mind off the present for a moment. Mikal shook his head. Now was not the time, not with what was happening inside the label. He couldn't believe his luck. Of all people, this woman had the craziest past he'd ever encountered.

Mikal's mind drifted to the day she woke him up with a blow job. That hadn't been disclosed to his friend. How could he, after the information she'd threw at his feet. He reached out and grabbed her hand. As secret as their love was, Mikal only wanted what was best for him. She knew that more than anyone else.

"Is there something wrong Mikal?" Ebonie asked.

He inhaled, taking that time to collect his thoughts. "What if your wrong?"

"I understand where you're coming from, but inside my bag is all the documents that Dr. Siriboe recorded. The man was obsessed with the outcome of her surgeries. He wanted to be with her. That's why I think she was involved with his death. No one knew about his allergies accept a choice few and she was one of them. All her theory session is in file because of the importance of the situation. I was there." Ebonie Johnson looked into his eyes. She could see his feelings floating in his face, to the point of sadness. "The procedures are long and draining for one reason...once the person commits, there's no turning back. They have to understand that."

Ebonie continued, "No investigation took place about Kofi's death because of the peanut oil in the food. They wrote it off as an accident. Candi was questioned, but that was it. If word leaks that she's not who she say's she is, her life will crumble, and she knows that."

Mikal let her hand go and turned his back. Every time he heard the words, it dug deeper into his soul. Copies of the papers were sitting in his office, where he'd left them after reviews. This had to be some type of Stephen King story. Ebonie stepped close and wrapped her arms around his waist. "I wanted you to hear it in person. It was surprising that she was a part of you label, but at the time I couldn't say anything. The night we spent together kept replaying in my head when you call and asked me to investigate this for you. I don't know why I didn't say anything then I'm sorry...I just didn't want to get involved until I was for sure." She rested her head in his back. "I don't know why she had anything to do with Kim's child. That should be the last thing she wants to do."

"Me neither. That's why I got some outside help. I can't let that happen. My life would stop moving. Let's go find out what's going on. I told Kim over the intercom that we were on our way." Mikal said.

When he turned, Ebonie stood on her toes and gave him a long kiss. "I'm glad we met Mikal."

"Me too, but from this day we can no longer be so open." He pulled her closer to him and winked. "I have a lot of things on my plate."

"That's always fun." Ebonie giggled.

They entered the room and walked to where Kim was sitting. She held her hands over her face, allowing streams of tears to run down her cheeks. Kim looked up when their footsteps neared. She rose and walked to Mikal. "He's back for revenge. I can't let that happen...not to my son." Kim laid her face in Mikal's shirt, then turned back to face Candice. To his surprise, she was sitting there with her hands untied. Candice averted her stare toward Ebonie as soon as she noticed her. No one else mattered. "How much did you tell him?"

"Everything." Ebonie replied.

"Mikal" Candice begin. "I'm sorry for what happened. I never meant for this to come into your life...I was just trying to keep my past hidden. I never knew anything about what took place. I told Kim the same." She begins to cry. Her swollen eye did little to her beauty. Looking at her, it puzzled him that this woman was once a man. No signs indicated that.

"Why didn't you just say that?" This world accepts people like you all the time. Why go through this madness to conceal the truth? Hell, we even have Donald Trump fo' president." Mikal smiled, trying to lighten the situation. Candice investigated her hands. "I wanted to live happily ever after like so many women. I wanted money, the big white house, and a handsome man like you. I had to make this work because it was so close. How could-..." She fell silent. Both women cut their eyes at him. Mikal was the ideal husband for many and this was a part of his problem now. He cleared his throat to get attention off him.

"Mikal, she says she'll help us get him." Kim added.

"Is that true?"

Candice nodded. Mikal looked around. "We won't have to chase you down, will we?"

"No, but I have to have your help also."

"That can be worked out." Mikal paused. "One more thing, you have to disappear, and nothing can be said about us if it blows up in your face."

"There won't be anywhere to go."

"Whatever the case, you have to go." Mikal said sternly.

"Why because- "

He broke in. "Let this be enough damage, please. I want your phone also...if you haven't already leaked the footage?"

Candice shook her head. "You're safe." She whispered.

Ebonie finally spoke after standing quietly through the whole ordeal. "What do you plan on using her for? Look at her face. She looks horrible."

Kim smiled. "We've had a long talk. That should make things better for us. Jeff is a smart man, but a rational thinker. He'll listen if we have some big chips to deal with." Kim walked toward the basement door. "I have people on their way to her daughter house as we speak. Candi's brother is married to her. It's a little bargaining chip."

Mikal smirked. This was something he wasn't used to, but Kim on the other hand came from this lifestyle. He asked. "So, what's the plan?"

"Stay close and you'll find out." Kim said, bringing a soft laugh from Candice.

CHAPTER TWENTY-FOUR

CANDICE

Children can be some of the cruelest animals in the world. Their harsh words honestly have denied people around them the opportunity to grow into the person that's deep within. Carlos was that boy. From the tender age of eight, his life was an aerobics cube. His feeling toward the same gender was confusing to him, but so normal. When boys played sports that gave them bruises and dirt stains, he elected to stay clean and fresh. None of those moments interested him. He focused on the way the little girls mingled amongst each other, the way they played house, the way they did everything. It was something about them. He could relate. Carlos would secretly hide in his mother's closet and dress in her clothing. He loved the way her oversized shoes looked on her feet.

Many days, he stuffed socks in her bras, so they would fit his chest when he tried them on. Carlos loved every second of his alone time. Carefully, he would replace her belongings just the way she had them, so no attention would be brought. Nobody could know how he thought about himself because there was no way to explain the feeling. It only matter to him how pretty he felt when he was dressed in woman's clothes. His mother was such a beautiful woman and Carlos studied her make up. The spark in his eyes, the feeling in his chest, the everything! Rosie Galvez was the one person that understood him, like so many mothers around the world. At times, when they were alone at home, she would allow him the chance to help her before leaving. "You must do this when your father's home, never." She would say with a kiss on his nose.

Those where the times that struck with him the most. Why hadn't he listened! Carlos remember the look in his father's eyes, the day he walked in the bathroom and found lipstick smeared across his lips. The slap his father gave his face had taken the breath out of him til this day. He left Carlos balled in the corner by the toilet, crying like the child he was. When father disappeared, moments later his mother appeared. "I told you never when he's here." Her whispers echoed. In his head he hadn't listened. Then the beatings begin. Jualian Galvez figured this was the way to strength out his son. No one accepted that in this country. He micromanaged his younger brother from that day forward, giving them little or no time to be together.

Even with those standards, Rosie encouraged him to be who he was. His father begins to care less and less as the calendar moved. Drinking became his getaway. Years passed, and his father begin to focus on his mother. She became the target of all his beatings. Many times, he wouldn't stop until she was unconscious. Then he would stumble towards Carlos room and give him that evil stare. It was impossible to know what would come next. That was too much excitement for his little chest. Then the call from school came. Carlos was caught behind the gym, bleachers, kissing a boy. His principal called, and his mother hurried to his aid, but to her surprise, the man refused to give way until he could talk to the father. Fear set in both their hearts; he was on his way. The beating his mother took sent them to America two weeks later.

Now Candice was in another dilemma, that involved her future and the well being of a child. What could she do to help this situation? There was no way she would be apart of anything horrific like that. A lot was riding on the line, with prison being at the top of the chart. She'd place too much time and money to throw it all away with her stupid choices. No, there had to be a plan for a plan. She stopped in front of the building and survived the surrounding area. It was a beautiful day to die. Slow traffic, bright skies, and cool breezes drew those thoughts. Candice knew there was people following her. That was the start of the plan. Mikal's word replayed to themselves. "You must leave. We'll be off the coast of Cuba when we receive the call that everything has been takin' care of. I'll know."

They were probably there at this moment. Candice entered the hotel and got on the elevator. A man entered three floors later with no words. They exited on the same floor but went in opposite directions. Her mind was to preoccupied to notice he was waiting in the shadows. She tapped and waited for the door to open. Her face was slammed in the frame of the door as it cracked, knocked her to the floor and catching Jeffery Hicks off guard. He had no time to reach for the gun tucked in his waistband. "Throw the gun to the floor Mr. Hicks and please nothing tricky, your daughter wouldn't like that." The stranger said. "Candice get up and shut the door before someone sees us." His eyes never left Jeffery Hicks. This was the same person who had entered the elevator. Mikal was playing a deep game. He steps to the left, entering the room more. "There's no one else in here I should know about, right?"

"No, I work alone." Jeff answered. "It's me and only me."

"That's good. No need to kill anyone else. My job was only you. Candice sit on the bed and make this call."

He gave her the number. "Tell them where we are at." Candice relayed the statement. "You want me to hand them the phone. That's what they're asking."

The man nodded. "Then place these restrains on him."

"Hello," Jeffery Hicks said calmly. As both gifts was given to him. "Is this some kinda joke?" He asked.

"No, it's real life and if you want her to live, you have to die, but we're fair it's your choice...someone's dying though." The man chuckled. "Kim doesn't want this problem to arise again. I can understand that. How about yourself?"

Jeffery Hicks investigated his hands. The game had sped up and he was left behind doing the same things. "I thought I could do this and be gone, but it's not the same anymore. A person must accept their wrongs when the times comes. That I've done. But you..." He pointed toward Candice. "...will not live in peace. I know your story and it's in the hands of someone special. What you've done will come to fruition...believe me. I'll see you in hell." He threw the phone to the floor. "Whenever you're ready."

"It won't be here."

I DON'T USUALLY DO THIS, UNLESS I'M DRUNK OR I'M HIGH, BUT I'M BOTH RIGHT NOW...

BOTH: DRAKE AND GUCCI MAN

"Aye boy what's good?" Mikal yelled through the receiver, as Kim lay next to him playing with her son, Jibril McDavis. He watched how she intensely focused on him. This was the call that would change their lives forever. It was the only way to end the drama and not be held accountable for the results. "Slick Rick tell me something good bro." The conversation lasted about ten minutes before he disconnected the line. "Well Miss lady, things have taken a turn fo' the better. All except Candi. "Mikal leaned in closer to smell her perfume.

That always eased his mind.

"What does that mean?" Kim asked.

"Some kind of way, she disappeared. They never planned to kill her, so a loose string was being kept on her. I only wanted to make sure she left the country, but befo' they could do that she vanished."

He shrugged his shoulders. "Maybe that's a good thing."

Kim sat quiet for a moment. "How's that a bad thing Mikal?"

"Because people like her tend to appear at the wildest times and the things she did to cover-up her past could be a lot crazier. I already must clean up the fact that she's not with the label anymore. Mikal rustled her son's hair.

She understood that better then he knew. Her past had traveled back and endangered the people around her. This was something Kim never wanted to happen. Reliving those times was hard enough. All she wanted now was to enjoy her life and watch her son grow up to be a man. "So where do we go from here?"

"Enjoyin' life and makin' records would be my guess. What do you think?"

Kim let her son free and watched him run around in the cabin. "That sounds good. Let's take a vacation. The music can wait. I just want to smile with you at

my side. I'll call Tracy and tell him. You take care of the other business. Deal?"

"I'll contact Live Nation and setup a tour fo' Secret Confessions, then we can have some fun." He leaned over and took her in his arms.

"Let's hope so." She started giggling. Kim couldn't remember the last time she'd been so happy. Then it reappeared. Viper would always be her first love. Watching Jeffery Hicks being sealed in a metal container had scared her beyond reason. She eluded them to escape. Her fear was being placed in the one beside him. The people they'd hired were killers of a different type. Punching holes in the sides and dropping him in the Gulf of Mexico said volumes. Candice had never witnessed that type of killing. She watched the video of her and Mikal. He had become her obsession. "All passengers boarding Flight 389 to Puerto Rico, please head toward the terminal now." Candice grabbed her single bag and walked that way. It was over for the time being, but she would be back, and they would know why.

18810075R00106

Made in the USA
Middletown, DE
08 December 2018